WHAT PEOP
CZECHMATE

MW00941547

Bridges' debut novel deserves five thumbs-up. First, I'm not a teen and I've never been a missionary in a foreign land, but I related to this story immediately. I read the book in one sitting because I didn't want to put it down. It was suspenseful and engaging, and thoroughly transported me to Prague, making me forget where I was actually sitting. Captivating characters are caught in multiple dynamic situations, centering on friendships, family interactions, challenges in faith, and even political intrigue. The total impact of the book—especially the heroine's undaunting desire to witness to others—will stay with you for days to come after you're finished. Best yet, you'll turn around and realize you learned a lot without even intending to. ~DL Koontz, author of *Crossing into the Mystic* and *Edging through the Darkness*

This isn't your sweet little missionary story. Bridges penned a romantic suspense that hooked me from the first page and would not let go until the last. A fast-paced adventure for readers of all ages! ~Vonda Skelton, author and speaker, Founder and Co-Director of Christian Communicators, LLC

I thoroughly enjoyed CzechMate, a young adult Christian adventure novel with more twists and turns, more ups and downs, more heart-stopping moves than a roller coaster. It's an edge-of-the-seat reading as the main character Nicole, her brother Adam, and new friend Jakub race through the dark streets and underground tunnels of Prague in a desperate attempt to rescue Nicole's parents from a Communist takeover. I loved how author Bridges used Nicole's strengths and weaknesses against her in order to grow her character. Nicole's eagerness and enthusiasm to share the Gospel (strengths) wind up hurting her and causing her to lose friends. Her dependence on others (especially her brother Adam and her friend Jakub) in times of stress would normally be considered a weakness. But that dependence is what causes her to trust God and ask for His help instead of blindly blundering into a dangerous situation, and becomes one of her strengths. Bridges brings to life, not only her characters, but also Prague, the book's setting. I felt exhausted at the book's conclusion, feeling as if I'd walked and run through this fascinating city with Nicole, Adam, and Jakub. You'll find CzechMate to be both thoughtful and thought-provoking as you hang on to your seat on this wild ride. ~Pam Zollman, Author and Speaker

I loved it. It combined all aspects of things I enjoy reading: a bit of adventure, a bit of mystery, a bit of just day-to-day life, and of course, God. This really was a great book for me, because I've moved to different places and lived there sometimes, so I feel her struggles over starting new schools and confusing languages.

This is a thrilling, enthralling book, chock-full with excitement and intrigue, while still carrying a truly wonderful story about God's glory. Sure to capture a reader's attention and hold it. They will smile, cry and learn along with Nicole about God's great plan.

An adventure story not only through the underground of Prague, but through the reader's heart as they discover God's careful hands carrying them through their struggles. ~Ning Soong, age 13

Edge of your seat excitement combined with faith in the face of adversity create a journey you'll be glad you took when reading *CzechMate*. Felicia Bridges' debut novel had me alternating holding my breath in anticipation and cheering for the characters as they learned that answering God's calling is not always easy, but always worth the cost. *CzechMate* is a great book for teens, and even not-so-teens like me. ~Tamara D. Fickas, contributing author to *God's*

Provision in Tough Times: 25 True Stories of God's Provision During Unemployment and Financial Despair and columnist for Broken but Priceless Magazine.

OTHER TITLES BY FELICIA BRIDGES

God's Provision in Tough Times – Contributing Author

Then Along Came an Angel – Messengers of Deliverance – Contributing Author

CzechMate

International Mission Force Series—
Book 1

Felicia Bridges

Madi,
May God lead
you on many
adventures!
Felicia
Bridges
Phil 4:8

Vinspire Publishing
www.vinspirepublishing.com

To Megan,
Your passion for God's mission inspires me.
Never doubt God's presence and power in your life.
He will equip you and guide your steps.

Chapter One

New Beginnings

"Nicole, it's time to say goodbye. We still need to get through Security before the flight leaves." Her mother's voice softly tugged her away from her two best friends, one of the two-legged and one of the four-legged variety.

She sniffed back tears and hugged Sam's neck for the fifteenth time. "Thank you so much for bringing Dobby to say goodbye."

"Don't worry about him. We will take really good care of him." Sam, her neighbor and best friend since first grade, picked up the floppy-eared mutt with eyes like dark, melty chocolates and let her sneak one more quick hug. Sam's red, watery eyes betrayed his jovial tone.

An airport security officer approached, his hand resting on the gun at his belt. Shooing Sam and his mother, along with Nicole's pet, back into their minivan, he urged them to move away from the curb. Nicole caught one more glimpse of Sam waving Dobby's paw to her out the passenger window before her mother pulled her into the airport terminal and hustled her toward the TSA checkpoint.

An hour later, the TSA officer finally released them. A family of four with eight overweight suitcases apparently posed a serious national security threat in his mind. Nicole and her family picked up their shoes and sprinted in their socks through the Raleigh-Durham International Airport. She glanced up at the sign listing the gate numbers and then her watch: ten minutes to go thirteen gates. Her rolling carryon clacked across the tiles as she and her little brother trailed their parents. A brief whiff of cinnamon as they raced past Cinnabon™ reminded her they had planned to have breakfast after they got through security. Her stomach whined.

"Wait! We're here! Please don't shut it yet." Her father waved his arms and called out to the uniformed attendant between gasps for breath just as she began to close the door to the jetway.

The woman pursed her lips as tight as the blonde knot on top of her head and tapped her navy Prada toe but allowed them to pass.

Four quick thank yous echoed down the metal corridor as they hurried past her. The second attendant at the door of the aircraft might have been her clone. She pulled the door closed behind them as soon as they entered the plane. "Please stow your carryon luggage and take your seats quickly to avoid further delays." Her emphasis on the word 'further' made it clear they were the cause for the current delay.

The other passengers glared up from their smugly seatbelted perches as the family jostled down the aisle to their seats in the back. The overhead bins were already securely latched.

Nicole's heart raced and breath came in deep drafts as she plopped into her seat by the window. She stuffed her shoes and coat under the seat in front, leaving her bag where her feet should be. She fastened her seatbelt and drew her knees up to her chin. Adam took the seat on the aisle and her parents sat behind them, all of them still breathing hard from their dash through the terminal.

Within minutes, the silver bird rocketed down the runway and heaved itself into the air. Nicole stared through the small window as the city where she'd spent her entire life dwindled to a gray smudge on the horizon. As the last wisp of smog disappeared and the altitude popped her ears, memories washed away her excitement for the adventure ahead.

Memories of concerts and competitions with the high school band. The faces of each of her friends as they gathered in the band room under a banner proclaiming, "We'll miss you, 'Cole!" Crying and laughing and hugging each other as they sang off key, "Na-na-na-na, Hey, hey, hey, Goodbye." Her drum set in the corner of the large bedroom she and Sam had painted last June. He'd helped her find the exact shade of teal as the ocean at Emerald Isle where their families rented a house together each summer.

As she reminisced about those childhood trips to the beach, the overwhelming sense of being tumbled head over heels under the surf returned. Sam's face as he waved goodbye. Dobby licking her face as she snuggled him close. The distance growing between them with each mile left a yawning emptiness in her heart.

She pulled the plastic shade down and drew her long legs into her chest, hugging her knees tight and burying her face.

"Why're you crying, 'Cole? I thought you wanted to move to Prague." The high-pitched voice prompted her to lift her head enough to glare at her little brother. The sympathy in his wide blue eyes made her stomach tighten and her jaw tense. She narrowed her eyes, warning him to mind his own business. She didn't want his sympathy. She didn't want anyone's sympathy. She did want to move to Prague. But that didn't make it easy.

The ten-year-old mumbled, "Whatever," and pulled his iTouch from the bag under his seat.

Nicole's forehead rested on her knees, and she pushed away the nagging sense that she should apologize. Adam was right, of course. That's what irked her the most. It had been six months since she and her father had returned from their two-week mission trip with the common goal of returning to the country they'd fallen in love with. It had been easy to win Adam's approval, but Mom had taken more convincing. When Charles University contacted Dr. Wise about their search for an Assistant Professor of U.S. Cultural/History Studies, even Mom could not deny God's hand in it. Despite Nicole's certainty that God had called her family to the mission field, doubt and homesickness gobbled up her confidence.

She had been so excited about the idea of leaving everything behind, she never considered she would be leaving behind everything she loved. In this moment, it was so not worth it. It didn't matter that her brother sat beside her and her parents were in the row behind them. She was alone in the middle of the ocean.

Lord, I wanted this, but it's so much harder than I thought. I miss my friends already and we haven't even landed. What if I can't make friends in Prague? What if I can't do this?

She sucked in the stale air and wiped her face one more time as she let the breath ooze out of her. She glanced through the crack between the seats to be sure her father hadn't seen her tears. Lips pressed firmly together, she vowed to herself not to complain, whine, or sulk.

The night dragged on as the plane soared over the ocean, the only sound the drone of the engines, the only light the tiny bulbs along the aisle and the glow of the screen in front of her. Adam dozed beside her, and a peek over the seat showed her parents snoozing too.

Really? How can they sleep? She flipped through the movie choices, barely noting the name before moving to the next, but none held her interest. Her fingers tapped a rhythm on the tray table until the white-haired man sitting in front of her turned around with sleep-filled eyes and glared. She glanced toward the window and folded up the tray.

Digging into her backpack, she pulled out the smartphone her parents had bought just a week before. If she couldn't bring her entire library, she could at least have a library at her fingertips, they said. Her finger tapped the app for her reader and then darted across the screen past tales of treasure, intrigue and mystery until it landed on one of her more recent downloads. She tapped the icon for the book of Czech legends and folklore, hoping to refocus on the future rather than the past. In moments, the captivating tales had whisked her away from the monotony of the flight.

Prague, Bohemia
March 12, 1577 anno domino
The stallion raced along the bank of the Vltava, sweat frothing on his withers. The young Emperor squeezed his knees into the ribs, easily guiding the beast up the steep hill toward the castle. His father had brought several fine animals back from the Imperial court in Spain, and the resulting breed boasted a majestic bearing, rounded head, and impressive stature. Rudolf could not recall any animal its equal during his years at his Uncle Phillips' palace in Madrid.

Only six months had passed since Rudolf had ascended to the throne following the death of his father, Emperor Maximilian II. At age twenty-four, his coronation met opposition. The Burghers, wealthy landowners of Bohemia, demanded an electoral process for identifying a monarch and he was only the second in his line to successfully inherit the throne. Fortunately, the Burghers were divided along religious lines, and their disunity weakened their attack on the Hapsburg line.

He found the pressures of ruling exhausting, and his only pleasure was escaping the court in Vienna to enjoy the remote solitude of Praha. He had left his attendants at the castle in Hradcany to follow the river as it meandered through the city, but even a race along the river failed to distract him today. Sweat soaked his forehead and gathered around his ruffled collar as he approached the castle. The black steed beneath him snorted and pawed the earth as he reined to a halt at the stable.

Wolfgang von Rumpf approached as he dismounted and the chamberlain's expression chilled the young man's blood.

"Your Excellence, I have news which must be discussed in private." The man refused to breathe another word until they had reached the castle. Once inside, Wolfgang dismissed the servants and spoke in hushed tones.

"Reports of a most disturbing nature have surfaced, Your Excellence. Several of the Burgher women have reported their children have been stolen. They claim the Jews have taken them." The man's dark eyes darted around the empty room as if the walls themselves were listening. "They use the blood to make bread for the upcoming Passover feast. The Burghers are demanding you renew your grandfather's decree that the Jews be expelled from Bohemia."

The young Emperor's knees weakened, and he sank onto a bench. The mantle of royalty weighed heavily on his narrow shoulders. His stomach lurched at the image the accusation painted in his mind and he tasted bile.

Wolfgang continued. "The Burghers are gathering in the courtyard. They are demanding an audience…and Your Excellence, I fear they could overthrow your rule if you fail to appease them. They want to know what you will do to protect their children from the Jews."

"Surely this is nonsense. They don't really believe such things…" But his voice trailed off as he saw the certainty in his advisor's face. He knew of the rumors. He'd heard them

often while at the royal court in Madrid. His own Great-great grandfather expelled the Jews from Aragon nearly a hundred years ago at the same time he first commissioned the explorer Cristobal Colon to find a faster trade route to Asia. His grandfather, the third in the Hapsburg line of Holy Roman Emperors, had twice tried to cast the Jews from Praha, but each time they seemed on the brink of ridding themselves of the troublesome minority, they seemed to return stronger and more prosperous than before.

But his imagination drew him to the other rumors he'd heard while at his uncle's court. Tales of mystical rituals and supernatural powers. Ancient secrets written in the Zohar and known only to rabbis. Perhaps this present challenge would provide an opportunity to uncover those secrets.

His thoughts of mysticism were interrupted by the roar of the crowd outside. The people would not be dissuaded. This would be the first test of his authority, and any weakness so early in his reign could easily prove fatal. He set his jaw and pulled himself up to his full meager height. One trembling hand smoothed his sweaty, ginger-colored hair away from his face.

"Summon the leader of these Jews. Tell those gathered in the courtyard I will resolve this directly."

Nicole jumped as the pilot's voice announced they were nearing their destination. Three flights, a long layover in London, and nearly twenty-four hours later, they had finally arrived. Lacing her fingers together, she stretched her arms and cracked her neck. She opened the shade to find the first orange rays of morning streaking across the sky. Homesickness dissolved into a glimmer of excitement as the sun peeked over the horizon. The plane started its descent into Prague, and she tucked her phone, the battery almost dead, into her bag.

The overhead lights snapped on, bringing the occupants of the plane slowly to life. Adam awoke and bombarded her with a steady stream of questions from the moment his eyes opened until they followed her parents off the plane. She tuned them out and answered through clenched teeth only when nodding or shaking her head didn't satisfy him.

Adam's chatter grated on her nerves, and it took forever to get through the line at Customs. When officials had finally cleared them, they dragged their eight large suitcases to the curb to wait for the hotel shuttle. Nicole shifted anxiously from one foot to the other, eager now to begin her new life. The January air burned going down her windpipe and puffed white clouds as she exhaled. Her warmest winter coat was no match for the wind slicing through it, and she rubbed her arms to keep them warm. What a difference six months made. It had been hot and steamy last June.

Resetting her watch to ten o'clock local time, she stifled another yawn. A deep breath yielded the unique blend of diesel fumes, sweaty, un-deodorized bodies, and exotic foods. *How can that possibly make me smile? But it does. Just like when I first gazed out at the red-orange tile roofs which formed geometric shapes all over the city. Homecoming. Crazy. How can it feel so much like home when I only spent two weeks here?* She gazed at the city, heart pounding, eyes tearing, but not in sadness this time.

"Nicole, let's roll." Her dad's hand waved back

and forth inches from her nose and then pointed toward the open door of the van where Adam sat on the bench seat.

She hopped in with a grin. Not even her annoying little brother could ruin this moment. She pressed her face close to the window and tuned out his incessant questions. The shuttle carried them past modern high rises and row after row of drab, cinderblock buildings, the ground floors covered with graffiti. Beautifully ornate, Gothic architecture stood next to Communist-era, gray concrete boxes. Ancient cathedrals shared the block with bars and tattoo parlors. Prague was called the 'city of a thousand spires,' and as they crested one of the hills, she could see them all.

The disparity mirrored her mood. Excitement and fear. Joy and grief. Love and loneliness.

She tore her gaze away from the scene outside the window to glance at her father. Adam and her mom had not been with them on the mission trip, so Dad eagerly pointed out sights like a little boy at the zoo. Nicole smiled. They both loved adventure. They both despised maps and lists and schedules. Those things were prisons confining her to a preset agenda, usually not one of her own design.

Her mom was the organized one. Mom never went anywhere without her planner. Moving to Prague was definitely not part of her plan. Nicole glanced at her mother and read the slight crease between her dark brows. *Worry. No surprise there.*

They'd searched for apartments on the internet before leaving the States, but the pictures they'd seen online bore little resemblance to the actual residences. There were plenty of one-room and two-room flats, but finding a furnished apartment with three bedrooms on an assistant professor's salary seemed impossible.

Each morning after eating the hotel's rendition of an American breakfast, they left with a realtor whose English was only slightly better than their Czech, and a long list of possible rentals. Eight hours later, which included a brief stop for lunch, they returned to the hotel disappointed. Each night, they drew a larger circle on the map and deleted one or two of their 'must haves' before selecting the list of possibilities for the next day's search.

On the fifth morning, she sat across the table from Adam for their morning ritual of boiled eggs, crunchy toast, and a cup of lumpy yogurt without the extra sugar and fruit she'd enjoyed in America.

Her father smiled, despite there being nothing to smile about in Nicole's opinion. "Today's the day. I can feel it. This is the day we find our new home." *How on earth does he stay so optimistic?*

"At this point, I'll move into a cardboard box…as long as I don't have to share it with Adam. One more day in a hotel room with him and I'm going to freak." She balled up her napkin and tossed it onto her empty plate.

"You're no picnic to share a room with either. And you snore! How many more apartments can there be in this city?" There it was again. That whiny tone drove Nicole mad. She folded her arms and rolled her eyes as she shook her head.

21

"That's enough, both of you. Where's your sense of adventure?" Dad glanced back and forth between them. Mom kept quiet.

After breakfast, they donned the new coats, gloves, hats, boots, and scarves they'd spent a fortune on—all required to combat the bitter cold and drifts of snow taller than Adam. They visited four flats in the morning, each worse than the one before. After a quick lunch of small, open-faced sandwiches called chlebíčky, their third stop loomed five stories tall, a white apartment building with a red-tile roof. As they trudged up to the building, the rows of balconies with alternating brick or frosted glass railings, gave it a more modern appearance than the peeling paint indicated.

"Look, it even has a playground." Adam grinned as he pointed at the dilapidated swing set like it was a ride at Walt DisneyWorld™.

"You call that a…" Nicole started to comment, but Dad's frown cut her short. After walking up four flights of stairs to the advertised apartment, she paused to catch her breath, tugging off the scarf.

"Have they never heard of elevators?" Her parents ignored her complaint as the realtor opened the door and stood back to wave them in.

"It is old, but they have done renovations," the woman explained in her heavily accented English.

Nicole followed her parents into the apartment, taking in the whole room in a single glance. A worn, plaid sofa, a chair, and an ancient TV on a rolling cart indicated this must be the living room. And the dining room. A small, round Formica table with four mismatched chairs consumed half the space. Beyond the table, French doors coated with multiple layers of peeling paint led onto the balcony. It wasn't fabulous, but it was the best they'd seen so far.

She wandered past the French doors and through the narrow kitchen, searching for the room which would be hers, the only room she cared about. Across the hall from the kitchen, the first bedroom included a double bed and built-in armoire covering one wall, but no closet. The double bed was a dead giveaway. This would be her parent's room if they chose the apartment. None of the apartments they had seen included queen or king-sized beds. Nicole wondered if they even sold those sizes here. She moved on to the next door. The bedroom was slightly bigger than her bathroom at home. *One tiny window, a twin bed with built-in bookcase and a small armoire. Adam's room…definitely Adam's room.*

She wrinkled her nose and turned to the final bedroom. *Please, please, pleeease, let this room be better.* She smiled when she saw the door onto the balcony which connected back to the dining area. *Sweet!* The room was the same size as the one with the small window and boasted exactly the same furniture, but the balcony made it perfect.

She stepped through the door onto the tiny cement slab and let the icy air cool her flushed cheeks.

Her mother's muffled voice broke into her moment of celebration. "It's tiny—the entire apartment would fit in our living room. The furniture is worn and outdated, but it will work. John, I'm not sure what you expected. I could have told you it wouldn't be easy, but I think this is the best we've seen within our budget." Nicole edged her way along the balcony to the doors by the kitchen.

Her parents sat at the kitchen table, apparently unaware of her presence. Her mom's jaw tensed visibly, and the crease on her forehead formed an exclamation point to her words. Her dad's head hung forward as if it were too heavy for his neck to hold upright. He seemed to be studying his hands clenched together on the table in front of him, his gloves stacked neatly beside them.

"Have I made a mistake dragging you all over here? I thought this opportunity was from God, but maybe it was just a coincidence. It all seemed to fall into place so perfectly, but now I feel like I'm asking my family to give up everything. What was I thinking?" His voice sounded strange and tight and quiet. Defeated. He leaned forward and rested his forehead in his palms as Mom reached out to touch his arm.

"It's not too late…" Her mother's voice softened and she let the sentence hang in the air unfinished.

Nicole's throat burned and she swallowed the lump that made it hard to breathe. She had to redirect this conversation immediately. She plastered on a huge smile and burst into the room as if she'd heard nothing.

"I love it! This is definitely the one. Can I have the room with the balcony?" She gave her dad a quick sideways hug and kissed him on the head as she danced around the table and back through the open door onto the balcony. "Look at this view." She left the door open despite the frigid breeze.

Bracing her gloved hands on the rail, she stood on her tiptoes. She could barely see the rust-colored roof-tops beyond the building ahead. Out of the corner of her eye, she saw her father wipe his face quickly as the real estate agent followed her brother back into the kitchen.

"Cool!" Adam ran to join her and stretched to see over the rooftops. She closed the door and smiled as her father asked the rental agent to sit down with them. While they worked out the details, she stood by Adam's side, pointing out the church spires which poked up over the sea of red.

CHAPTER TWO

A Rough Start

Nicole smiled as she stacked her books in the bookcase on the headboard of her bed, her victory in the battle for the balcony still fresh. A couple of touristy posters of the Astrological Clock and Charles Bridge brightened the naked walls, and a small bulletin board featuring her Varsity letter and Best New Marcher Award reminded her of home.

She crawled into bed and gazed at these scraps of her former life, the aching hole threatening to open in her heart again. She rolled over to face the posters and reached for her phone. Texting Sam before falling asleep wrapped her in cozy familiarity as she lay awake, adjusting to the sounds of the city.

The morning dawned bright and clear, with the sun beaming through the panes of glass in the door blinding her. She knuckled the sleep from her eyes and pulled the pillow over her head to block out the offensive light.

"Nicole!" Her mom's voice carried through the small apartment, a prelude to her throwing open the door and bouncing on the edge of Nicole's bed. "Time to get up. We're going to visit Prague International Church today."

Nicole yawned and pushed feebly at her mom, mumbling in protest as she curled into a ball. Her mother tugged on the pillow for a moment, then left her to get ready. She waited as long as she dared before slipping out from the warm covers into the chilly morning. By the time she had dressed, breakfast was on the table and the rest of the family had started eating without her.

"There she is. I thought we might have to roll your bed down the street to take you to church." Her dad laughed alone at his joke.

"That sounds like a plan to me." She turned as if to return to bed, but Mom interceded.

"Oh, no, you don't. We need to leave in about ten minutes, so you need to eat up." She set a plate of eggs and bacon in front of her.

Nicole crunched through two pieces of bacon before starting on the eggs. By the time she'd finished, the other three were waiting by the door.

The family lumbered down the hill in their new polar-bear-style winter coats as Nicole described the church they had served with while on the mission trip.

"It's so cool…it's on this busy street, but you go through the doorway into a hall leading to a little courtyard, and that's where the actual church is. It shouldn't be too far. I think we got off at the stop called Jiriho something or other."

Her father glanced at the paper he'd written directions on. "Jiriho z Podebrad." His North Carolina drawl converted it to Jerry-ho Zee Potty-brad.

"As if I know any more now than I did a moment ago." Her mother laughed as she adjusted her scarf to cover her ears.

"They meet at the Czech church, but upstairs, they have a service in English. There are people from all over the world." Breakfast had provided some quick energy, and Nicole was eager to see if any of the friends she'd made on the mission trip were there this morning.

"Ha! The only ones you're interested in are boys," Adam taunted.

Nicole shot her brother a wicked glare.

"Can we please not fight on the way to church?" Mom stretched her arms toward each of them like a referee overseeing a boxing match.

Dad laughed as usual. "Now what fun would that be? It wouldn't be Sunday morning if the kids weren't arguing about something."

"John, don't encourage them." Now, Mom was scolding Dad, but only playfully. By the time they'd finished their teasing, they had reached the station.

They eased into a row of folding metal chairs at the back of the room as the congregation began to sing along with a young man strumming a guitar from the small platform in the front.

Nicole craned her neck and scanned the room, but from behind, it was impossible to recognize anyone. Her mother pursed her lips and shook her head, nodding toward the stage to draw her attention back to the service. When the music faded, Pastor Michal stepped forward to speak. She smiled and resisted the urge to wave at the familiar face.

Pastor Michal read from 2 Kings, relating the story of Elijah and encouraging them to realize God's presence and authority over any situation. Nicole listened, but her mind wandered back to memories of her previous visit. Their mornings were spent visiting secondary schools and speaking with the students about life in America, letting them practice their English skills, and trying out phrases they'd learned in Czech. In the afternoon, they had gathered in a different park each day, performed a quick puppet show for the children in the park — with the soundtrack recorded in Czech — and then talked with those who came to see the puppet show with the help of an interpreter. Afterward, they'd gone to dinner together and then wandered through the historic Old Town before returning to their hotel.

Nicole's mother tugged on her arm, bringing her back to the present, as the music began again. When the pastor dismissed the congregation, she and her family greeted Pastor Michal.

"It is so good to see you again, my brother." The pastor grabbed her dad's hand and pumped it enthusiastically. "I did not expect to see you again until this summer."

Her dad smiled. "I didn't expect to be able to return so soon — or for it to be on a more permanent basis, but God opened the door for me to teach at the university through an exchange program."

"Ah! You are here for good, yes? That is wonderful!"

"Well, at least for a year."

"And you have your whole family with you, I see."

The pastor turned to her mother with a smile.

Her father introduced her mom and brother and added, "You remember Nicole from our visit last summer."

"Of course! It is so good to see you again, Nikola." She loved the way he converted her name to the Czech pronunciation.

As they stood talking, the room emptied quickly until they were the only ones left. A young man moved through the room, folding the chairs and stacking them against the wall until the room echoed with their voices. He approached the pastor and interrupted the conversation hesitantly.

"Please excuse me. Pastor Michal, is there anything else I should take care of before I leave?"

"No, thank you, Jakub. You are such a blessing to me. Let me introduce you to my friends — Jan and Marie, and their daughter, Nikola, and son, Adam. Friends, this is Jakub, my young assistant." The pastor pronounced the name "Yah-coob." The teenager stood as tall as her father, his dark hair in uneven strands over his forehead. He glanced around the circle with a quick nod to each before retreating without another word.

"He's not much of a talker, is he?" she muttered as she watched the door shut behind him.

"You must be patient with Jakub. He is learning to trust us. The police forced his family to leave the apartment they had been staying in last fall. Their utilities were cut off. One of our families heard about their situation and offered them a place to stay. We have been trying to simply show them the love of God, but it is difficult to reach beyond generations of distrust and mistreatment."

"What do you mean?"

"Jakub's family is Romani. For centuries, they have been persecuted and abused, treated as second-class citizens...no, even worse, they have been treated as not even human, let alone citizens. Many people know that the Jewish people were exterminated in Hitler's camps, but few realize the Romani people were also annihilated. The population of Romani in the Czech lands was less than six hundred, by some counts, by the end of World War II. Unfortunately, in the years after the war, Slovak and Hungarian Romani immigrated in such numbers they were seen as a threat. Fear leads to hate and keeps them from being accepted."

"That's terrible, but it was so long ago. What does it have to do with them having a place to live?" Nicole glanced again at the door.

"Romani are seen by some as unfit to employ, and they keep to themselves and their own communities. They are often forced to move and then condemned for being shiftless nomads. They are denied the basic dignities of life, and then accused of being dirty. Because they speak and teach their children a form of Czech that is easily recognizable and doesn't follow traditional rules of grammar and pronunciation, their children are identified as having special needs, placed in special schools, and denied a full education. Then they are ridiculed as uneducated. In this case, they had taken residence in abandoned tenements which were barely fit for humans. The laws which are intended to ensure minimal acceptable living conditions were used against them. They were forced out of these places that were unfit to live in, but provided with no other place to live."

"I had no idea. Is there anything we can do to help?" The crack in her voice betrayed her mother's soft heart.

"We tried to offer places for more of the families, but it is difficult to earn their trust. Jakub's family alone accepted our help, but not our friendship. His parents have avoided us. But Jakub spends hours each day with me, helping in little ways…putting away chairs, sweeping the floors…even mopping the water closet. I think, perhaps, he sees it as earning what we have provided, though I've told him he owes us nothing. I would ask only one thing of you. Please pray for him and for his family."

Nicole felt like her mother sounded, heartbroken for the injustice. "We will definitely pray for them."

They spent Sunday afternoon preparing for their first day in their new school. Mom endlessly rehearsed the Metro schedule and insisted they travel to every single stop to practice finding their way home. She warned them about pickpockets and purse-snatchers and declared that Nicole must wear her apartment key on a string around her neck in case her backpack was stolen.

It hadn't been easy to convince her mother she could ride the Metro alone to school. Her mom had been determined to go with her until she realized it was impossible. She had accepted a job teaching art at the elementary school, thinking the kindergarten through twelfth grade Hillside International School was in a single location. It turned out the high school was in Hradcanska and the elementary campus was three miles north in Sedlec. Classes started at the same time, but her mother had to arrive early and her father had a class at the University. The only option was for Nicole to do what the children in Prague did from elementary school on—ride the public transportation alone.

She hid the key under her shirt, hoping no one would notice. She grinned and glanced at the people around her on the Metro as she headed toward school for the first time. Her pulse danced at having won a little independence.

Nicole popped her knuckles through her thick gloves as she emerged from the station and made the hike from the metro station to Hillside High School for the first time. Three blocks in the freezing cold. Three blocks which filled her with excitement and dread. Riding the subway alone thrilled her, but starting a new school halfway through her freshman year in a foreign country…not so much.

The old, single-story school building with its white stucco and ubiquitous red-tiled roof smelled of new paint, disinfectants, and student lunches. Not so different from home, although the aroma from the cafeteria was more inviting.

There was some comfort in the knowledge that her classes would be in English. After six months of practice before they left, she knew just enough Czech to be dangerous. Her hands were shaking. *Breathe*, she reminded herself. *This is it. My mission field.*

She entered a cauldron of students jostling one another and chatting in Czech, but not one made eye contact. The single hallway made finding her first class easy enough. She bee-lined straight to the back of the room and scooted into an empty desk. A quick glance confirmed the classroom was similar to back home. Rows of desks, a board at the front, and posters on the walls. At least that much was familiar. No flat screen TV, and no iPads for the students, though. Her fingers tapped a beat on the desk as she watched students pour into the room. A girl with black hair and thick eyeliner shuffled in and sat beside her.

No time like the present.

"Hey, my name's Nicole." She raised her hand in an awkward wave and smiled.

"Mara." The Goth chick waved back and then looked down. *Conversation. That's what I need to do, make conversation. But how?* Words eluded her.

"Are you from Prague or did you move here from somewhere else?" Clever.

"Prague is my home. My father is a Senator." She only had a little accent, but her English sounded stiff and formal. Nicole had read that the students at Hillside were either the children of foreign diplomats or of the wealthy elite. Only her mother's job as an art teacher allowed her and Adam to enjoy the pricey private school.

What else can I ask? Lord, help me think of something to say! The teacher called the class to order. *Thank you, Lord!* The teacher's voice faded to a drone as she spent the class searching for an intelligent comment to make.

But when the class ended, Mara left without another word.

Nicole searched for her all day, but no luck. And no one else seemed interested in anything she had to say either. By the end of the day, her face ached from forcing a smile.

Okay, God, what is up with these people? They don't want anything to do with me. She shuffled toward the metro station, discouraged, until she noticed Mara up ahead. She picked up the pace and dodged through the crowd to reach her.

"Looks like we're headed the same direction," Nicole said as she fell into step beside her.

Mara smiled. Sort of.

"So, tell me about your family. I have one little brother named Adam. He's a real pain." She rolled her eyes. *Aren't annoying younger siblings a universal truth?*

"I have no brothers or sisters." Her voice was flat and her face expressionless.

Fail. There must be more to her story, but better not push it. Try a different topic. "We moved here from the United States. My dad is a visiting professor at Charles University, but we really came here as missionaries."

"Missionaries?" Mara's black brows flew up and her eyes grew wide.

Finally, a reaction. Nicole hesitated, not certain if Mara's reaction was surprise, anger, or enthusiasm. Maybe she should explain. "We came to Prague to tell people about Jesus."

Now the chick's whole face glowed pink and her dark eyebrows met in the middle of her forehead. "We know about Jesus. Do you think we don't study history?"

Nicole panicked. *What do I say now?* "Oh, I know you know about Jesus—but you don't know Jesus. We want to tell people about why Jesus came. He came to save them from their sins."

"What?" Mara stopped and stared. Her face was a red balloon about to pop. *Not good.*

Nicole's evangelism training kicked in and the words tumbled out in a desperate bid to calm the irate girl down. "Have you ever thought about if you were to die today, where you would spend eternity?"

Mara stared at her, her lips a red slash and her eyes narrowing. Nicole's face grew hot under her glare. She opened her mouth to speak, but the other girl spun on her heels and stormed off without another word.

So much for making friends and winning people for Jesus.

Nicole threw open the apartment door, tugged off her boots and parka, and tossed her bag on the sofa. An hour to kill before her mom and Adam would get home. She needed to warm up after the cold trek from the subway station and cool off from her encounter with Mara.

I want to punch a wall. No, what I really want is to pound out my frustration on my drums. But they're 5,000 miles away. Who am I to think I could be a missionary? My first try, epic fail.

She plopped down beside her bag and yanked her books out to start on homework. Maybe homework would take her mind off Mara.

By the time her mother and little brother arrived, she'd finished her homework, but her mood had not improved. Adam dropped his book bag by the door, saying, "I'm going to hang out at the playground." He darted out the door before her mom could answer.

"Be home in an hour," her mom called to him as the door slammed behind him and she sat beside Nicole on the sofa. There was that crease again.

She definitely knew something was up. *How does she always know?*

"So how was your first day of school?"

No point in hiding it. The story of her miserable failure came gushing out and ended with, "I am such a loser." Her thumb and forefinger formed the monogram 'L' on her forehead for emphasis as she flopped her head back on the sofa.

Her Mom's arms wrapped her in the smell of clean cotton. "You are not a loser. You're just a little too passionate for your own good sometimes. I know you want to tell people about Jesus." Her mother stroked her hair as if she were five. "But you also have to be careful. Remember, we're in a foreign country. You need to take time and get to know people before you start talking to them about why we're here. You can't just spring it on them the very first day." Her mom pulled back and stared into her eyes. "You don't know who these kids are."

The worry lines between her brows were a little deeper now.

"I know." Nicole stared at the purple laces on her tennis shoes.

Her mom kissed her on the forehead and rose from the sofa. "You're going to have to get to know Mara and the other kids. Earn their trust and learn who you can trust," she said as she walked into the kitchen.

Her mother was right, but it hurt to know she might have done more harm than good. *From now on, I will think before I act. No more rushing in before I have all the facts.*

She reached for the book of Czech legends. Perhaps tales of intrigue and the supernatural would distract her from her failure.

Prague Castle, Prague, Bohemia
March 29, 1577 anno domino
The Rabbi entered the Emperor's throne room with shuffling feet and downcast eyes. This would be his first audience with the Emperor and he certainly hoped his last. It was best for God's chosen people to avoid the notice of the Emperor. Although Emperor Rudolf remained neutral in the continuing battle between Catholics and Hussites, the Rabbi was uncertain his objectivity extended to Jews as well.

"Halt!" The Emperor's voice stopped him in his tracks and he refused to raise his eyes lest it be perceived as disrespect. "You are Rabbi ben Loew?"

"I am Yehuda Leow ben Bezalel, Rabbi." His voice barely carried across the space of the cavernous hall, and his gnarled hands gripped one another.

There was a long pause, long enough for the Rabbi to pray for Yahweh's protection and guidance, before the Emperor spoke.

"*I have heard reports about you. Reports that you prac-tice mystical and ancient arts.*"

The Rabbi's head snapped up and he found himself gaz-ing into the eyes of the most powerful man in the world. He quickly returned his gaze to the hands clenched before him.

"*I study the Tanakh, the Torah, Nevi'im, and Ketuvim. Perhaps these are the ancient works you speak of.*"

"*Perhaps. What do these works tell you?*"

"*They teach us about Yahweh, Almighty God, creator of heaven and earth and all that is in them.*" *Did the Em-peror truly want to know about the Torah?*

"*And what does the Zohar teach?*"

The Rabbi bowed his head deeper. "*It teaches the Kab-balah – but only to those prepared to learn.*"

"*And does it teach you how to create as Yahweh does?*"

Again, the Rabbi reacted without thinking, this time staring at the Emperor for several long moments before an-swering. "*It teaches us we must not seek to counterfeit the work of God.*"

The Emperor's face flushed and the Rabbi knew his ad-monition had not been well received.

"*And what do they teach you about killing children? Do they teach you to steal a mother's child in the night for your evil sacrifices? Do they teach you the recipe for using their innocent blood in your bread?*"

The Rabbi fell to his knees at the accusation as if he'd been struck. It was not the first time they had been accused of such atrocities. Josephus had defended them against such accusations fifteen centuries ago – even before the followers of Yeshua began joining with others in the ridiculous claims. If they had any knowledge of the Torah at all, they would understand he dared not even be in the presence of a corpse

lest he become unclean. Certainly taking a life — and espe-
cially the life of a child — was a violation of all he held sacred.
He inhaled the musty air of the castle and raised his face once
more, this time resolute.

"It is against every tenet of our faith to commit such an
act. Our God would surely not allow such an abomination
among His people."

The Emperor watched him closely, the flushed color fad-
ing slowly from his face.

"So you deny it?" he asked finally.

"I tell you, it is not true."

The Emperor stared at him, but the Rabbi locked his
gaze on that of the younger man and refused to back down
this time.

The next morning, Nicole waited resolutely on the
steps of the school, searching the crowd for Mara. Her
thumb tapped the rhythm from the song in her head
on her leg. For the fiftieth time, she checked her watch
and then gave up and hurried to class as the bell rang.
The seat beside her in her first period class remained
conspicuously empty.

Her stomach churned as she headed to second period — Geometry. Her hands quivered and she stared
at the floor. She sank into a seat in the back and wished
she could disappear, but the girl in front of her turned
around and introduced herself.

"I am Eliska." The girl covered a heinous smile
with her hand.

Flashback to her own smile before braces. Ouch.

"I'm Nicole." She grinned. Maybe her reformed
smile would encourage the poor thing.

"You are from America, aren't you?" Eliska stammered a little and continued to talk through her hand.

"Yes, we've only been in Prague a week. We came from North Carolina." *Whoa. Don't go there again.* She glanced away and bounced her thumb on the edge of the desk. *Change the subject. Now.*

"Have you ever been to America?"

"I would like to go to America one day. I want to see New York City."

Eliska's uneven smile faded when she confessed she'd never been to New York. The teacher called the class to order and she relaxed. *No major blunders. Whew.*

Eliska trailed her to her next class, her voice a consistent drone along the way. Nicole must have been too frazzled the previous day to notice that Eliska shared all her classes except for her first period English class. After Geometry, they sat through History and then followed the stampede to the cafeteria. Eliska hammered her with questions about the United States as she picked at the food on her tray. For the first time since arriving, homesickness tugged at her heart as she talked about her school, her friends in the Marching Band, and the small city where she grew up.

With her memories consuming most of her attention and Eliska hogging the rest, they were dumping the remains from their lunch trays into the trash can when she noticed the other students staring at her and Eliska. Some narrowed their eyes and whispered to each other. Some lifted their chins and cocked their heads to one side, their noses slightly wrinkled as if studying an insect. But they all stayed a good distance away from Eliska at all times. *Creepy.* She shook it off and followed her new friend to their next class.

Eliska talked non-stop between classes and sometimes during the classes too. The incessant chatter irritated Nicole, but at least she had a friend now, she told herself. Eliska stuck closer than a brother. And not in a good way. By the end of the day, Nicole fought against the temptation to stuff a sock in the girl's mouth.

Nicole rushed out of the school. Maybe Eliska hadn't seen her. She hated to avoid her only friend, but she couldn't take another word. She hustled down the slushy sidewalk to the metro station, ignoring the crowd. The train pulled into the station just as she reached the platform, and the tide of people washed her toward the open door. In her desperation to escape, she didn't hear the bell warning passengers of the closing doors. The people around her surged toward the congested train, but the doors shut in her face.

"Really?" She ground her teeth and stomped her foot. Nothing she could do but wait for the next train. It was already 4:00 pm, and it would take thirty minutes to reach Djevicka. She tried to stay close to the edge of the platform. When the train came, she pushed through the mob trying to exit. She could not miss the train again. Sitting near the door, she pulled her book bag into her lap and rested her head on top of the bag.

Lord, how can I witness to these people when most of them won't even talk to me? And what kind of missionary runs away from the people they are trying to witness to?

"Mara wasn't in school again, but I met a girl

named Eliska." She resolved to see the glass as half full as she stood at the sink washing dishes and handing them to her father to dry. At home, she had regularly complained about having to spend ten minutes loading the dishwasher, but somehow, with her father standing beside her, she didn't mind washing them by hand now.

"That's wonderful, 'Cole. I knew you'd make some friends. I had some good news today, too. I talked with the principal of one of the Czech elementary schools and they are willing to have me come in and speak to the children to help teach them English."

"Awesome, Dad." Nicole raised a soapy hand for a high-five.

Her dad smacked her hand, sending bubbles all over both of them as they laughed.

"And I talked to a friend on the Missionary Council and he told me about something which might make things a little easier on you." He grinned as if he had a special secret.

"What is it?"

"Nope, not gonna tell you. I'll have to show you when we get finished."

She rushed through the dishwashing and teased her dad by standing with arms crossed, tapping her toe while he dried the last plate and put it away.

Finally, he brought his laptop to the kitchen table. "I know moving has been hard for you, especially giving up your computer. And I can't let you use this one for playing games or surfing the web all the time because it's the only one we have, but I don't mind if you use it sometimes." He signed on and typed in a URL before swinging it around to face her. "It's a message board for missionary kids. They call it the International Mission Force. Bob said his kids love it."

"Wow, Dad, that is great. Thanks. You have no idea how much I miss having a computer of my own." She smooched his cheek and sat down to check out the web page. A list of message topics filled the screen, starting with a note about rules for posting. She scanned the text and set up a profile with her name as CzechCzick, then posted a message under the topic 'Introductions.'

Hi. I'm Nicole. I'm 15 and an MK in the Czech Republic. We're brand new to the mission field and I could really use some help! So far, I've made one girl so mad she hasn't been back to school in two days and I made friends with another girl who is driving me nuts! Help!

She scrolled down to a thread about 'Adjusting to the Mission Field' and read through three pages of messages. Some of the messages were vague, but one near the bottom of the third page hit home.

I've been an MK for six years, and we've lived in three different countries. For me, the easiest way to adjust to a new place is to spend time exploring the area. When you travel around the city and learn where everything is, it feels more like home. 2Tim314.

That sounded like a great idea. She typed in a quick response: *2Tim314 – thanks for the suggestion. You really have the MK thing down. Where have you lived?* She hit enter and went on to read several more messages before a chirp indicated an answer to her message. She scrolled quickly to read the message.

CzechCzick – Welcome to the MK message board!

Yeah, I've definitely been around a while. I've lived in Japan, Thailand, and now we are in the same general area — can't talk about where we are now — It's not easy but it is worth it. Don't give up! I saw your intro post too and I know what it's like to mess up. We all make mistakes so don't let it get to you. 2Tim314

A smile touched her lips.

Chirp.

Another message popped up. Within thirty minutes, she received ten messages from MKs all around the globe. She spent the next two hours getting to know them. There was GRACEKIDS which was actually two sisters, one fifteen and the other thirteen, in Bolivia; MK2SK, a thirteen year old boy in South Korea; 14Jesus, a sixteen year old girl in South Africa; and 2Tim314, an eighteen year old MK who couldn't reveal his location. Each of them shared stories of their own mistakes, and pretty soon, she didn't feel like such a failure anymore.

She stretched and yawned, rubbing her weary eyes. The clock on the computer read 11:00 p.m. and a quick look around the room showed she was the only one still awake. Posting one last message to each of her new friends, she closed the computer and went to bed.

Chapter Three

Second Chances

Nicole stood guard each morning on the steps of the school, drumming her thigh anxiously as she watched for Mara, eager to apologize and start fresh. Three days later, she finally returned, but Nicole was there waiting for her.

"I'm really sorry. I know what I said the other day was, well, kind of insulting. I didn't mean to insult you." She shifted her backpack from one side to the other.

"It is fine." The girl's black eyes darted back and forth and she continued into the school without pausing.

"Friends?" She smiled and extended her hand, trying to match Mara's pace.

"Friends…" The girl whispered as if they shared a secret. She did not touch Nicole's hand.

Weird. But she didn't have time to push for more. They were at the classroom.

Mrs. Cervenka droned on for forty-five minutes about writing a five paragraph essay while Nicole searched for the nerve to ask Mara to join her for lunch.

When their English class ended and they moved into the hall, she tapped her shoulder. Mara winced and jerked away from her hand. Her black-rimmed eyes seemed filled with pain as she blinked back tears and then darted through the crowd. Nicole's stomach twisted in a knot as she imagined possible explanations. Her next two classes were a blur of her own emotions mixed with Eliska's chatter.

Another lunch with Eliska. Ugh. She scanned the lunch room and wished she could sit at any other table. Mara and her friends sat across the room, laughing. Eliska's table was a dull island in a sea of fun. She thought about her friends back home and longed to be with her band geek buddies instead of trying to answer Eliska's endless questions about America. The thought of spending lunch at this table for the rest of the year was torture. Her fingers tapped on the edge of the table as she wondered how to escape. She glanced back at Eliska who sat across from her with eyebrows raised.

"I'm sorry, I didn't hear you." Her cheeks grew warm.

"I said, 'Why did your family move to Prague?'" Eliska smiled her awkward, irregular smile as she repeated her question.

Smart. Better pay attention next time. Need to think on my feet, not get caught off guard.

"Uh, yeah. My dad's job brought us here." She bobbed her head. It was the truth. Sort of.

Nicole arrived at their apartment and hid in her room until her mom called her for dinner. She sank into her chair with a dejected thump. Her dad gave thanks and asked God to bless their food and give them strength for ministry. *Ministry. Right. That's why I'm here. Sigh.*

"What's wrong?" her mom said as she passed a plate of fried chicken.

Nicole stabbed a leg with her fork and passed the plate to her father. "Mara came back to school today and I apologized, but I don't think it did any good at all. And Eliska is driving me nuts. She talks all the time and it's always questions about America. Really? I mean, what am I, the Encyclopedia Americana?" She rolled her eyes.

Her father chuckled. "So the missionary life isn't quite what you imagined it would be?"

She studied her plate. "Yeah, I guess. I thought it would be easier than this. And more fun." She wrinkled her nose.

"Well, I think Prague is great!" Trust Adam to pipe in just about now. "I've made a bunch of friends, and so far, none of them have stopped coming to school because of me." He pushed a large forkful of green beans into his mouth.

She rolled her eyes again and picked at her food as he continued, despite having his mouth full, to expound on his new friends throughout the meal. After washing the dishes, she pulled out the laptop and logged on to the International Mission Force message board. A post from 2Tim314 requested prayer for a family whose home was burned to the ground because they offered bibles to their neighbors – that really put her struggles into perspective.

Why do people always respond to things they don't understand with cruelty and violence?

Josefov, Prague, Bohemia
April 25, 1577 anno domino
Rabbi Ben Loew sat at his table, a candle illuminating the scroll before him. His wife placed a goblet of wine beside him before retiring for the night. He often spent hours writing by the flickering light of a candle. His wife had long ago accepted his obsession.

His head drooped as the candle burned down until a loud noise roused him. Flickering light danced down the street toward his home as a crowd approached carrying torches. With trepidation, he lifted the stub of candle and went to the door as the rowdy crowd arrived.

"Friends!" What irony that he would call them such. "Please allow me to help you. Whom are you seeking?"

The crowd turned as one to face the old man. The bloodlust in their eyes reflected the moonlight, and the Rabbi shivered despite the warm spring evening. A gaunt, dark-haired man wearing the clothing of a Burgher stepped from the crowd.

"We want the ones responsible for our missing children. If you hand them over, we will not harm anyone else. If not, we will burn your homes to the ground."

"Please, we have not done this terrible thing. Our law forbids us to kill. I wish I could help you, but the one you seek is not among us." The Rabbi spoke in a loud voice, hoping to reach each one in the mob with his reason.

He could hear them grumbling between themselves, growing more restless as the moments passed. Their self-ap-

*pointed leader glanced at his followers and motioned for si-
lence before responding.*

*"Of course you deny it! But our children are gone." He
motioned quickly to three of the men near him. They ran to
the nearest home and heaved their torches onto the thatched
roof. It immediately burst into flame, sparks dancing up into
the black sky. The crowd dispersed quickly, lighting other
fires as they went.*

*The Rabbi ran after them, screaming for his neighbors,
calling out to God for help. But the heavens were silent except for the sizzling and popping of the inferno.*

Nicole prayed daily but weeks passed with no
change. Mara remained distant despite her attempts at
conversation. Eliska continued her daily interrogation
about all things American, and Nicole somehow found
the patience to answer her questions without explod-
ing.

Her thoughts wandered toward self-pity as she
leaned her head against the window of the train, her
fingers tapping on her knee. The metro approached
Hradcanska, and she yawned and stretched as she
stood to exit the train. She had stayed on the MK message board until midnight, reading about 2Tim314's
brush with danger and the hundreds who professed
Christ at GRACEKIDS' rally. She yawned again for the
second time in five minutes.

The escalator carried her to street level and the
three-block trek through the snow to school. Wrapping her arms tightly around her middle, she pushed
forward against the icy wind and stepped over piles of
slushy gray snow. She mentally rehearsed what she

would say to Mara this morning. Maybe she should ask about – *smack!*

The sound sliced into her thoughts and jerked her head toward the alley beside her. A deep voice shouted in Czech just ten feet away as a man towered over a crumpled figure on the ground. He yelled again, and she struggled to make sense of his words. With one hand, he jerked the figure to her feet, and Nicole recognized the black hair immediately. A flash of Mara's tear-streaked face sent her rushing in without another thought.

"What are you doing? Leave her alone!" she yelled as she stormed the alley.

The bully spun around with a menacing glare. She couldn't understand his slurred speech, but she gasped when she saw his face. She'd seen him before...part of the crew at Mara's lunch table.

Mara quickly moved between them with her hands up. "Please. It's all right. You go now." She pushed at Nicole, urging her to leave.

"It is not all right. Did he hit you?" The red imprint of his hand on the girl's face answered her question. She stared over her friend's head at the bully. He stood over six feet tall with tousled brown hair and pale skin. She had seen him across the cafeteria, but up close, his dark eyes were glassy and bloodshot. His fists were clenched and ready to fly again. She shivered and grabbed her friend's hand.

"Let's go. We're going to be late for class."

Mara didn't resist but peeked over her shoulder several times. When they reached the school, she pulled away.

"That's my boyfriend, Slane. You should not have interfered." Her eyes were wide with fear.

Nicole stared at her and shook her head. She paused a moment, trying to comprehend her reaction, and then followed her into the bathroom. Mara wiped at the mascara streaks on her face with a coarse paper towel. Nicole waited until she couldn't stay quiet any longer.

"He shouldn't hit you. It's not right."

Mara gazed into the mirror and made eye contact, raising her brows. She focused her attention on re-applying her make up as she spoke. "You don't understand. You come here with your plans to 'save us,' but you don't even know me." Her voice cracked and her hand shook a little as she put on red lipstick.

Nicole rocked back on her heels. "I'm sorry. I want to know you better, but you won't let me in. Besides, nothing would make it right for your boyfriend to hurt you. You should tell your mom about this."

Mara tipped her head back and let out a hollow laugh. "You see? You know nothing!" She spun around and locked her gaze on Nicole, their faces inches apart. "My mother is dead."

Nicole's mouth gaped. She caught sight of her stunned expression in the mirror and stared at the floor. *Talk about putting your foot in your mouth.* "But your father...you said he's a Senator. He wouldn't allow someone to hurt you, would he?"

Now her chuckle sounded low and throaty. "No, he would not." She paused for a moment as if considering the possibilities and then smiled—a cold smile which didn't reach her eyes and sent a chill up Nicole's spine. Without another word Mara tossed the paper towel in the trash and left her standing alone.

She moved through the cafeteria line, dreading another interrogation. But as she turned from the cashier with her tray, Mara grabbed her elbow and led her to the table she had longed for the day before. The table usually occupied by Mara's circle of friends...and by Slane. She called out names quickly as Nicole set her tray on the table. Ondria sat on Rubert's lap and fed him bites of food. Her hot pink hair and edgy fashion made Nicole feel like a sparrow next to a peacock. The lovebirds cast a quick glance at her and then ignored her and the other members of the clique. Tynek and Izak appeared identical, both blond and blue-eyed, but Tynek towered over Izak and everyone else. Their chiseled good looks belonged on a movie screen.

She lifted her hand in a feeble, awestruck wave. *Smile. Act normal. Breathe.* They nodded briefly in greeting and then produced a deck and started dealing cards while they munched. She sat beside Tynek and watched them play a game which looked like War. *This is it. I've escaped the isolation of being an outcast.*

Slane appeared as she took her first bite. Her mouth went dry and the normally delicious food suddenly tasted like sawdust.

He grabbed Mara and kissed her roughly. "Omlouvám se."

She choked on her dumpling at his mumbled apology.

Mara pulled away from him and sat beside Nicole with a look that dared him to move her. The lanky brute took the seat opposite Nicole and glared at her. She met his gaze and lifted her chin. *I'm not afraid of you, you big jerk.*

Mara chattered away about their classes, the weather, and her plans for the summer. She must have been trying to hide her nerves, but Nicole noticed her friend's hands were shaking a little as she picked at her food. Ignoring the brown eyes riveted on her from across the table, she focused on the conversation. Until she saw Eliska sitting alone. She should invite the other girl to join them, but one thought stopped her. *I don't want to go back to exile.* As Mara talked, Nicole's conscience battled her pride.

When Mara paused, her conscience momentarily gained the lead. "Do you know Eliska?" She gestured toward the redhead.

Mara laughed. "Everyone knows Eliska."

"What's that mean? Why does everyone avoid her?" Pride gained ground and urged her to be cautious in her support of the outcast.

The Czech girl paused as if deciding how much to reveal. "Her father is General Ruzicka. He is Commander of the Army in Czech Republic."

"And that's why no one speaks to her or sits with her?" It seemed like a strange reason, but a lot of things seemed strange about her new friends.

"No. He is also former KGB — Committee for State Security. They moved here from Rusko — Russia, you call it. They are all spies. No one trusts her." She waved her hand dismissively as if sharing simple common sense.

Nicole's mouth dropped. She had been sitting

with the girl for a month and didn't know her at all. Maybe Mom was right. She needed to learn more about these people before she opened up. Relief that she had not revealed their reason for moving to Prague flooded her mind.

When the lunch hour ended, her conscience drove her to Eliska.

"Hey, sorry I didn't join you for lunch today. Mara asked me to sit with her."

Eliska continued walking without a word.

"Really, Eliska. I'm sorry. I don't want to lose you as a friend, but Mara is my friend, too."

Eliska spun around and Nicole saw the tears waiting to fall. "My father was in KGB, long ago, before I was born. I know what they say. They make up lies about me."

"But I don't believe that. Really, I don't." She couldn't decide what to believe, but the look on Eliska's face sliced through her heart.

The girl gazed away and blinked back tears before Nicole continued. "Can we still be friends?"

Eliska shrugged and stalked off without a word.

Nicole sat in History class and tried in vain to give Mr. Kohout her undivided attention. Her thoughts wandered between how to help Mara escape her dangerous relationship and how to make amends to Eliska. She stared out the window at the soccer — football — field, searching for a solution. The pencil in her hand thumped a beat on her History book.

"Ms. Wise? Excuse me, Ms. Wise? Perhaps you can explain the significance of the Velvet Revolution?" Mr.

Kohout interrupted her thoughts.

"I…uh…no, sir. I can't." Her face grew warm and her mind drew a complete blank. If he had asked for her name, she would have been equally speechless.

He drew a long sigh as if she had personally offended him. "Class? Can anyone explain to Ms. Wise the significance of the Velvet Revolution?"

Eliska raised her hand and Mr. Kohout beamed.

"The Velvet Revolution is significant because unlike most revolutions, the demonstrators advocated for freedom from communism peacefully. Nearly 15,000 students gathered at Vysehrad and began marching toward Wenceslas Square, carrying only flowers to give away. But when they reached the halfway point, they were blocked by police with sticks who beat them. In the end, democracy prevailed without any lives being lost." She glanced over her shoulder with a smug expression.

Nicole sank lower into her seat, hoping Mr. Kohout would ignore her for the remainder of the class.

When the final bell rang, she searched for Mara and found her waiting for a bus at the crowded bus stop.

"So what are you going to do?" she whispered.

"What do you mean?" Mara shifted her books in her arms and stared at the ground.

"About Slane. You can't let him keep hitting you. Please tell your father." She grabbed the girl's arm. "Tell someone."

Mara glanced up and met her eyes for a moment. Nicole caught a glimpse of the battle between fear and some other emotion she could not identify. She wished she could do something more.

The moment dragged on. Mara finally broke the silence. "I will think about it." The bus arrived, belching diesel fumes, and she watched her friend climb aboard and disappear.

Lord, help Mara tell her father.

The next morning as she rode the escalator up from the metro, Mara rushed to meet her.

"I did it." The girl's voice whispered intensely, her eyes wide.

Nicole knew immediately what she meant. "You told your father?"

She nodded briskly. "You were right. He was so angry. He told me Slane won't hurt me anymore." Her voice trembled.

"I'm so glad you told him. You don't have to worry about Slane hitting you now."

"Thank you. If you hadn't stopped him yesterday, I don't know what would have happened. He got so furious with me, but then he would apologize and beg me to forgive him. I was too afraid to say anything." She shook her head as tears welled up.

Nicole put her arm around the other girl's shoulder and squeezed gently. "It's going to be all right. Everything is going to be just fine now."

"I hope you are right. My father was irate." Her relief seemed tainted with an edge of fear.

The day passed quickly as Nicole bounced from class to class, energized by a sense of accomplishment and pride. Not even the cold shoulder she got from Eliska could dampen her enthusiasm.

At lunch, she went straight to Mara's table and confidently took her place. *If Eliska doesn't want to forgive me for having lunch with them, then she can sit by herself.* The usual crowd gathered with one notable exception. Slane was absent.

CHAPTER FOUR

Baby Steps

Four months later

The Wise family sat near the front of the sanctuary as Pastor Michal presented a sermon pulled from two stories about Samaritans: The Good Samaritan from Luke 10 and the Samaritan Woman in John 4. As he described the strained relationships between the Israelites and the Samaritans, she cast a glance across the room to where Jakub lingered in the doorway. Each week, she caught him listening when Pastor Michal preached—never coming in and sitting down among them, but lurking in the shadows as if afraid he might be caught.

The tapping of Adam's feet as he swung them back and forth, slapping the worn hardwood floors, stole her attention. She nudged him to stop his fidgeting only to have her mother elbow her and hold a finger to her lips as if she were the one creating a disruption.

The service ended with a song and then the family

meandered toward Pastor Michal who greeted his congregation as they departed. Nicole glanced around the church, but Jakub seemed to have vanished. Her parents were speaking to Pastor Michal as Adam shuffled from one foot to the other, complaining about his stomach growling.

"Pastor Michal, how is it going with reaching out to Jakub's family? I noticed him again, hanging out by the door. Why doesn't he come in if he wants to hear the sermon?"

The pastor glanced around and lowered his voice. "Honestly, I believe the boy is drawn to the gospel. God is working. But his family remains distrustful. You must pray for him. Pray, too, for our people, that they would welcome him."

"But the church has been so welcoming..." her mother started.

Pastor Michal cut her off. "They have welcomed you, but welcoming someone like Jakub is much more difficult. There are hundreds of years of history to overcome, on both sides. Even when their hearts tell them to love someone, it is not easy to keep their hands and their mouths from acting as they have for generations."

Nicole restrained the urge to skip along the now familiar route from the Hradcanska metro station to Hillside High School. She stopped at the news stand for some candy and popped one in her mouth as she soaked in the early morning sunshine. Only two weeks until summer vacation.

Mara darted out of the alley, the same alley which

had seen the birth of their friendship, and glanced both ways before grabbing her arm and pulling her into the shadows. Her face was red and puffy. "I have to talk to you!"

"What's wrong?" Nicole's pulse raced. Despite the months which had passed, her first thought flew to Slane. *Has he finally returned? Has he attacked Mara again?*

Mara's eyes darted anxiously. "My father is very angry. He found the Bible you gave me and he said I cannot be friends with you anymore. He hates the West, and he sees only the bad things which freedom has brought to our country. And he does not believe in God."

"I'm so sorry. I didn't mean to get you in trouble." She hugged her friend and breathed a sigh of relief. Compared to her wild imaginings, an angry, overprotective father seemed harmless.

"It is not your fault. I wanted to read this Bible. I wanted to know what it said for myself. I have been reading every night before I go to sleep." Her excitement seemed to overcome the fear of her father.

Nicole could barely believe her ears. She had begun to give up hope that her friend would ever understand or even desire to understand the things of God.

A chill danced up her spine, and for a moment, she contemplated pushing Mara, encouraging her to pray for forgiveness and salvation. Instead, she hugged her again and said, "Don't worry. I'm sure your father will get over it."

Her friend pulled away and met her gaze with a

strange, sad look, tears welling up. "For now, we cannot be seen together. Nicole..." She paused and her face twisted in pain. She glanced again around the alley and finally spit out the words like poison. "I think my father did something to Slane. No one has seen him for months. It is safer if he thinks we are not friends." Mara rushed out of the alley before Nicole could answer.

She stood in the alley, her hands hanging limp and her mouth open. The alley began to spin around her before she remembered to breathe. She stumbled to the wall and steadied herself against the rough bricks. Mara's final words ripped away the joy of learning she'd read the Bible Nicole gave her. Her heart ached with loss that congealed into a knot of anger. Rage painted frightening images of revenge in her imagination. Was there anything she was not capable of?

Josefov, Prague, Bohemia
June 1, 1577 anno domino
Rabbi Ben Loew stood over the freshly turned earth and spoke words he hoped would comfort the aching hearts of the people gathered to say goodbye to twelve-year-old Estreilla. His fists were the only hint to the turmoil and rage that brewed beneath his calm visage. The fires had burned out of control through the night, and when the morning light dawned, her parents discovered Estreilla's frail body amid the ashes of her family's home.

He ground his teeth and waited until the mourners had moved away before approaching his daughter's husband. His strong grip on the younger man's arm conveyed the intensity of his anger. When he was sure they would not be overheard, he revealed his plan.

"Josef, we cannot allow this to continue. They plot against us – burn our homes and kill our children – we must find a way to defend ourselves against these monsters!"

Josef was a peaceful man by nature, but the death of the little girl had shaken him out of his normal complacency. "What will you do, Rabboni? Whatever it is, you will have me beside you."

The old man patted his arm, thankful for his unwavering support. "It is good to know that I can count on you, Josef. I must study and pray. Perhaps God will show me a way."

The two of them filed quietly out of the small cemetery and followed the procession through the narrow, muddy streets to the synagogue.

The day passed in a torturous procession of classes where Nicole discovered that, along with Mara, all the relationships she thought she had built were strained. Mara's status among her classmates ensured that anyone she shunned, they did likewise. She had returned to those first miserable days…a stranger and an outcast once again. The day which had started with such joy fizzled into a dreary reminder that she was not in control.

With dinner and the dishes finished, she pulled her father's laptop from its bag and settled into a chair at the kitchen table for some needed encouragement from her online friends. She pulled up the forum page and posted a quick message about her friend, Mara. Within minutes, the chirping sound of the notification encouraged her.

GRACEKIDS: *Praying for you!*

1Tim314: *It's going to be OK. He'll get over it.*

MK2SK: *Wow, that stinks! I will say a prayer for you too.*

Venting to someone who knew her pain helped so much. By the time she went to bed, she was sure tomorrow would be better.

Nicole slumped at a table in the corner of the cafeteria. She might as well have been in Siberia. It had been three days since her sentence of solitary confinement had been imposed. Every now and then, she caught Mara's eye and recognized the sympathy and friendship that lingered. Small comfort when she sat here all alone.

"This seat taken?"

She jumped at the sound of a voice directed toward her. *Eliska. Outcasts united once more.* She mustered a smile.

"By you." She pulled the chair out as the redhead set her tray down.

An awkward silence stretched between them as Eliska sat and began to eat. Finally, Nicole couldn't take it anymore.

"Listen, I'm sorry for abandoning you before. And I'm sorry for the way everyone treats you."

For a moment, she wondered if she'd spoken out loud. The silence stretched awkwardly as Eliska kept her head bowed as if she hadn't heard. Finally, she met Nicole's stare with tears brimming. "I forgive you."

"Why? Why should you forgive me? I was awful to you."

She shrugged. "People do bad things. But they can change and do something good if you give them time."

CHAPTER FIVE

First Fruits

"Breakfast is ready. Please hurry. I need to talk to you before you leave for school." Her mother's voice carried through the small apartment as she finished her quiet time. A slight edge in her voice spurred Nicole on. She scanned a few verses of scripture and prepared for school in record time. Her stomach roared as she slid into her chair and poured herself a glass of milk. Her mom set a plate of warm pastries filled with apples and cinnamon in front of her.

"Thanks, Mom. You know I love kolaches!" She bowed her head and gave a cursory but sincere prayer of thanks before taking a large bite of the pastry that was one of her favorite things about their life in Prague.

The crease between her brows, which Nicole hadn't seen since shortly after they arrived, replaced her mother's usual smile. She opened her mouth to speak, but Adam interrupted.

"What's for breakfast?" He rubbed sleep from his eyes as he wandered to the table in his pajamas.

"M---m!" Nicole tried to protest, but her over-loaded mouth couldn't get the words out. Her brother snorted with laughter, which only infuriated her more. When she had washed down the bite with a gulp of milk, she complained, "Mo-om, he's not even dressed yet. He's going to make us late, and I wanted to meet Mara this morning!" Spending precious moments with her friend before school helped her survive the past two weeks of banishment.

"Don't worry. Your father has prayer meeting at the church this morning because of the election, so he is going to drop your brother and me off on his way. You can leave as soon as you're ready and walk to the Metro yourself today. He won't make you late. So slow down, you have plenty of time. But we do have to talk before you leave."

Her dad appeared in the doorway. "Have you told them?" His worried frown matched her mother's.

"Told us what?" Nicole jumped in. *Something definitely up.*

"Let's tell them together." Her mom crossed the kitchen and slipped her arm behind his back, leaning her head on his chest. She sighed. That small sound spoke volumes.

Her father's silence made her stomach tighten as he made eye contact. "Nicole, of course I'm happy your friend is coming around. We wanted to share our faith. That's why I took this position with the University and why we came to Prague." He spoke slowly, choosing his words deliberately. "But we need to be careful. Some of your friends at Hillside have parents who are powerful politically. You know Mara's father is a Senator. From what I've been reading in the papers, he's not receptive to allowing missionaries in the country, so I'm glad we are here with the University. We need to pray for Mara. But we also need to pray about how we can help her without endangering our family." She had never seen her father so disturbed.

"John, I know we might have to leave, but do you really think we could be in danger?" Her mother's voice mirrored his concern.

"Leave? We can't leave now!"

Her father raised his hand to silence her protest.

"Things are changing, and not for the better. The Communist Party holds a minority of seats in the Senate, but they've been campaigning strongly for today's election. Many people are unhappy with the changes freedom brought to Prague. They see casinos popping up all over the city, 'adult' magazines at every news stand, and satellite TV telling them what Westerners, especially Americans, are like." He shook his head, his lips pressed into a thin line, before continuing. "Some would rather have Communism. Learning to work hard to gain the things they want in life is difficult. They grew up with only the bare necessities of life and were taught not to hope for anything more than that. Now, they have to work hard to have even those basics, and yet they see others around them sometimes gaining much more."

She could barely believe her ears. "Dad, do you think they would choose to go back to Communism?"

"I don't know, honey. Even after five months, I sometimes don't understand these people at all. People prefer oppression to freedom because freedom requires responsibility. We need to pray for God's will in this upcoming election. If the Communists return to power, we could be forced to leave the country. Or worse." He glanced toward her mother who had returned to the table.

"So we need to pack some things, just in case. We'll pack a change of clothes in some of our grocery totes. This way, we're prepared." Her mother had a plan for everything.

Nicole's heart sank at the thought of abandoning their new home so quickly when she finally saw God working in her friend's life. She let out a disappointed moan, just this side of whining.

"But we can't go back now." The tears came before she could hold them in.

"We have to trust that if God allows the Communist Party to gain control of the Senate, then He has a plan for that. It is not going to take God by surprise. Right?" Her father prompted.

"Right." Not very convincing.

"He knows we're here. After all, He called us to serve here. We have to trust Him to protect us and allow us to keep reaching people as long as possible. Right?"

She sniffed a few more times before letting out a muffled, "Right."

"And if we are forced to leave, then we've accomplished His purpose for us being here. We have to trust that He will use the people we touched to reach others. Remember, it's not about us and what we want or even what we think is best." He caught her gaze and held it.

"We're here for as long as God wants us to be here, to do what He wants us to do. Right?"

"You're right. I know you're right." She sniffed, her shoulders lurching as she sought to catch her breath and regain control. Her father took her hand and pulled her out of the chair into a hug. "It's so hard to imagine." Her words were muffled by his shirt.

"I understand how tough this is. But this is an opportunity for us to lean on God." He hugged her tighter, patting her back. "I don't want you to worry about this, 'Cole. Always remember, we're safer in a war zone if it's where God wants us than back in the States if we're out of His will."

Maybe it was cliché, but it made her smile.

"Better?" Her father kissed her forehead.

She nodded. "Thanks, Dad."

With a renewed sense of urgency, she sat down and devoured a second pastry. More eager than ever to capture any possible moment with her friend, she put her dishes in the sink and slung her backpack onto her shoulder. Her mom met her at the door.

"Before you go, I need you to pack a change of clothes. Just in case, remember?" Her mother gave her a canvas bag, and she went to her room and stuffed it with a change of clothes. When she returned to the kitchen, she found her mother standing in front of the cabinet.

"We don't want to look like we're going anywhere out of the ordinary." Her mother placed a box of macaroni and a can of tuna in the top of Nicole's bag so it would look like a grocery bag.

My mother plans for every possible disaster, but really?

All the secrecy is overkill, even for her.

"Mom, this is ridiculous. We don't need to be all '007' about this. I mean, what is the big deal? Why would they even care about us? Dad is a History professor. You're an art teacher."

Her mother shot her a quick look, and she decided resistance was futile, so she dropped the bag on the sofa and stepped to the door for a quick hug and a prayer with her mom, their morning ritual before parting ways for the day.

Her mother began. "Abba Father, please be with Nicole today. Protect her and give her wisdom. Help her especially to be your witness to her friends. Keep our family safe while we're apart and may your will be accomplished in this election."

"Lord, thank you for all you're doing in my life," continued Nicole. "Thank you again for giving me such a great friend and help me to lead her to you. Protect her from her dad's anger. Forgive me for not being a better friend to Eliska and help me to be more patient with her. Lord, please don't let anything happen with the election that would make us have to leave. Amen."

She gave her mom a peck on the cheek and slipped out the door before her father finished his morning devotions.

She arrived at Hradcanska forty-five minutes early and waited anxiously for her friend in the space behind the tiny grocery store. As the minutes ticked by, Nicole paced the narrow alley. Where was she? Her mind flashed back to the first time they'd met here.

The day Mara had told her father about Slane's abuse. No one had seen Slane since that day.

The memory did not reassure her. Nicole drummed her leg with her thumb. She shuffled, head down, eyes following a crack in the pavement. Peeked around the corner. Checked her watch again. *No sign of her. Where could she be?* The fear on Mara's face when she told Nicole that her father might be responsible for Slane's disappearance haunted her. *Could he really be that evil?* She shuddered at the revenge she had envisioned. Was she really any different? Finally, she gave up and sprinted for the school. *Maybe Mara is sick.* Just when it seemed like God was doing something amazing, human weakness and sin got in the way.

Prague Castle, Prague, Bohemia
June 18, 1577 anno domino
The Emperor slammed his fist on the table, making his silverware jump and clatter as they landed. His servants scattered, accustomed to his periodic outbursts.

"How can I maintain order and direct my attention to the more important matters of state when these religious fanatics are bent on destroying the city in the name of their god? Am I not the King of Bohemia? Am I not the Emperor of the Holy Roman Empire? Find these miscreants and bring them to me! There will be consequences for their disrespect." *He stood and upended the table before storming from the room.*

Chamberlain von Rumpf watched the violent reaction in stunned silence. He knew the Emperor held no affection for the Jews — nor for Catholics or Protestants for that matter. Having a Protestant father and a Catholic mother, Rudolf had grown to loathe them both. He favored his own unique worldview, one that worshipped science, mysticism, and the occult more than any god.

Puzzled at the Emperor's apparent and uncharacteristic concern for the welfare of the Jews, he followed the Emperor from the dining hall to the Lion's Court where the Emperor stood admiring his prize. Mohamed, a mature African lion, paced back and forth in the small enclosure. At the Emperor's nod, a servant tossed the carcass of a skinned deer into the hutch. The Chamberlain shuddered at the smile on the Emperor's face as he watched intently while the beast tore it apart and devoured it.

Nicole darted through the crowds at the school like an antelope avoiding a predator. The bell finished ringing as she loped across the room. She sank into her seat, wishing she could sink right through the floor. She tried to catch her breath as whispers swirled around her. Glancing around the room, she realized the gossip was not about her late arrival.

Every eye seemed to bore a hole in her heart.

Some seemed gripped with fear. Others seemed angry. Their eyes narrowed. Their upper lips curled in disgust as if she were a cockroach. Yesterday, she'd been shunned. Today she was despised.

As the teacher began the lesson, she tapped Ondria's shoulder and whispered, "What's up? Did I grow a second head or something?"

Ondria tossed a glare over her shoulder and shook her head. "It's Mara," she said through pursed lips. "Her father is moving her to a different school because of you. I told her she should never have trusted you."

Nicole's heart fell. Her eyes burned, and she pressed her lips into a grim line and willed herself not to lose it right there in class. The teacher spoke, but she only heard Ondria's words echoing in her mind. She moved from class to class in a daze, barely aware of the teachers or the stares and whispers of the other students.

With her mother's warning that they might be forced to pack up and go home ringing in her ears, she drank in the experiences which had become commonplace. The guttural sounds of Czech conversation in the hall, now familiar and mostly understood. The glimpses of red roofs through the tall windows. At lunch, the pungent aroma of Czech dishes simmering in the kitchen.

Out of habit, she started toward the table she had shared with them up until two weeks ago, but Ondria faced her with arms folded. She glared at Nicole as if daring her to sit at the table. Rubert, Tynek, and Izak gave her an uncomfortable glance and then avoided her. She ducked her head and turned away.

She searched the room for an empty table and finally found a spot in the corner. Even Eliska seemed to have deserted her today. The first bite of the usually delicious goulash seemed to lodge in her throat. *I won't see Mara anymore. The one real friend I made in all this time.* She was alone. But even more than simply being alone, she had failed. Failed miserably, just like that first week. It had taken five months to build a relationship with Mara to the point of giving her a Bible, of seeing her interested in any aspect of Nicole's faith...and now every inch of ground she'd gained was lost.

When the final bell rang, she lumbered toward the Metro station. She kept her gaze riveted on the ground, her strength focused on not dissolving into a puddle of tears. The escalator carried her from the bright June afternoon into the darkness of the station. She shuffled from the escalator to the platform.

A shove from behind sent her flying toward the pavement. She barely caught herself a split second before her face hit the concrete.

Gasping to catch her breath, she pushed herself onto her hands and knees. Ondria, Rubert, Tynek, and Izak surrounded her. Ondria stood tapping one foot, her arms crossed once again. She spat out a foul word in Czech, and Rubert snickered. Izak's eyes darted around the platform, and Tynek shifted from one foot to the other.

Can I hope for any mercy from them?

"You could not leave her alone, could you? Even after she told you she wanted nothing to do with you anymore," Ondria said in Czech. "Always talking about Jesus. 'Jesus loves you.'" Her nose wrinkled in disgust. "You had to keep pushing Mara until she joined your religion, became a Christian." She sneered as if the word were profane.

"Mara hasn't…I mean. I don't think she is—"

"No!" Ondria cut her off. "Save it for someone who believes your lies. Her father told my father last night how you brainwashed her. She even tried to convince her father to convert." Her foot flew toward Nicole's gut where it landed with a thud. The air whooshed out of her lungs, and she gasped like a fish out of water as she tried to suck some back in. Curling into a ball around the pain in her stomach as her tears broke free, she gulped for more oxygen.

Ondria murmured, "See how much Jesus loves you now?"

A pair of shiny black shoes clacked across the platform toward her, offering a glimmer of hope. She scanned up slowly to see crisp navy pants and shirt, a silver badge, and a stern face beneath the dark cap. The Metro Security officer blew his whistle, scattering the gang. He swung around as if to follow, but allowed them to escape and came back to Nicole instead. Her rescuer reached down and took her hand, pulling her to her feet.

He asked about her injuries, and she answered in broken phrases, her mind struggling to think in Czech as she panted. The boot had caught her just below the ribs, leaving her sore, but nothing seemed broken. Her heart was another matter. How could they turn on her so quickly? She stooped to brush the dirt from the platform off her jeans and pick up her backpack. But when she stood to thank the officer, he had vanished. She surveyed all around and up the escalator. No sign of him. The skin of her neck tingled.

What if they came back? Her jaw tensed. The station grew crowded with commuters headed home, but would anyone help her if her attackers returned?

She stepped toward the edge of the platform and allowed the breeze that preceded the train to cool her warm cheeks. The doors opened, and a sea of humanity poured out. She scanned the crowd. Would the gang follow her? She looked again but didn't see them. Rushing onto the train before the last people exited, she picked a seat where she could watch the door.

Nicole clutched her book bag in front of her, trying not to cry as her stomach ached. Her mind rewound the day and played it back again and again. Each time she saw Ondria's foot coming at her, she felt the kick once more. Her memory trapped her in an endless replay of a bad movie where she played the victim.

"Malostranska!" The voice blared from the speakers, rescuing her from the torture. Strangers around her rushed off the train, only to be replaced by new strangers. She peered around in confusion as the doors closed and the train gained speed once again. The next station was Vysehrad—two stops past her neighborhood. She'd been so lost in thought, she'd missed her stop. Her mind raced through the metro map, thankful for once for an overprotective mother who'd insisted she know every route by heart. She mentally calculated the best way to get home and then realized she'd almost missed the next station as well. At the last moment, she squeezed out, moving against the press of those trying to enter the train. The underground air tasted stale and thin like the ancient air in a tomb, and she had to escape.

Elbowing her way through the crowd, she reached the escalator. She could catch a bus down the street that would carry her within four blocks of home. The Vysehrad station stood near downtown Prague, and crowds were gathering on the sidewalks as she emerged from the station. The area teemed with people most of the time, but the mood today seemed different.

Instead of moving purposefully toward home or work, oblivious to those around them, the people wore tense frowns and milled about in small groups. They spoke in hushed whispers she could not get close enough to hear. The bus stop stood a block from the Metro, across from the Congressional building, and she struggled to push through the throng on the steps which had spilled over the sidewalk onto the street. Traffic beeped, but the pedestrians merely ignored them and the drivers slowly merged to ease around the mass of people.

Nicole arrived at the bus stop as the number 58 was pulling away. *Twenty minutes until the next one.* She edged closer to the couple beside her and tried to listen to the conversation, hoping to understand the shift in mood. *Does it mean trouble for our family?* Her mind jumped back what seemed like a week to her mother's concern this morning. The woman spoke to a man beside her in angry tones, her words the rapid staccato of machine-gun fire. *Is it my imagination or did the woman say "communiska"? And is that good news or bad news for the Communists?*

It took forever before the bus arrived, and Nicole boarded quickly, moving to the back near the rear door. She stood, even though there were seats available, and gawked out the window. A man climbed to the top of the steps in front of the Congressional building, shouting and waving his fist in the air. With his dark suit, slick black hair, and mustache, he looked like a cartoon villain. She exhaled slowly, relaxing a little as the bus pulled away.

She watched as a crowd joined the man on the

stairs, shouting and waving their arms while others shook their heads and walked away. As the bus rounded the corner, three police cars rushed toward the scene, their sirens blaring the odd 'weeh-wohh' she had grown used to.

The bus deposited her four blocks from the flat. Here, life carried on as usual. Whatever the trouble, it seemed confined for the moment to the vicinity of the Congressional building. She hurried up the hill toward home. Taking the stairs two at a time, she raced to the apartment and locked the door behind her. She leaned against it for a moment to catch her breath as she tossed her backpack on the sofa next to the bags they had packed this morning. *A million years ago.*

When her heart stopped racing, she stepped into the bathroom and lifted her shirt above the waist to inspect her injury in the mirror. She stood on her tiptoes to see her belly in the small glass hung over the sink. The toe of Ondria's boot had left a mottled purple oval just below her ribs.

She pulled her shirt down and caught sight of her face. Her eyes were huge and scared and outlined in red. Twin streaks of white cut through the blush on her cheeks, and her dark hair tangled wildly around her face, framing it and making it that much paler by comparison. Her mother had freaked out enough this morning about the whole election, she didn't want to add the problems with her friends to the mix. Mom couldn't see her like this. She didn't want to re-live the attack by telling her mom about it. And she certainly didn't need Adam's comments, whether they were teasing or pitying. She pulled a brush through the snarls in her hair, washed her face, and reapplied her make-up.

When she could see no more visible evidence of her ordeal, she plopped on the sofa and clicked on the TV. Her first choice was CNN. It was the only station in English and her only source of current information for stateside news. She hoped they would report on the election in Prague, but the program focused on US national news. It didn't take long to catch up on the same old news back home. Wildfires in the West, threats of tornadoes and flooding in the Plains, and a tropical storm which might grow to hurricane strength and threaten the Southeast. Her friends back home came to mind, and she whispered a quick prayer for their safety. There were political stories, which were of no interest at all to her, and a missing person report about a little girl who had disappeared from her front lawn. She muted the TV to pray again, this time for the young girl's return.

Satisfied there was no good news from home, she flipped to the local station. Of course, they broadcast the news entirely in Czech. She'd learned enough of the difficult language to carry on a conversation with anyone patient enough to speak slowly, but the rapid-fire speech of the announcer made it harder for Nicole to understand. She watched the channel mostly to expand her understanding of the language. She could usually piece together the gist of the story by catching an occasional word and watching the film clips.

Today, the story centered on the election, judging by the picture of a ballot box beside the news anchor's head. A graph showed the breakdown of the results and she gasped as she realized the cause for the commotion downtown. She didn't know if the demonstrators were celebrating the results or protesting them, but the unofficial results were in.

The Communist Party of Bohemia now controlled the Senate.

CHAPTER SIX

Captives for Christ

Nicole stared at the television in disbelief. Her worst fears were confirmed. She flipped through the channels, searching for an explanation.

Finally, CNN picked up the story. News anchor Megan O'Hara smiled as if reporting the local weather. She explained that out of the ten contested Senate seats, nine had been won by Communists, giving them a slim majority in the Senate according to exit polls. Although the official election reports were not in, the Communist Party seized control of the government in anticipation of a victory. News clips of the same scene she witnessed on the steps of the Congressional building identified the ringleader as Vladimir Novak, leader of the Communist Party of Bohemia and Moravia, and the presumed President of the Senate if the Communist Party indeed had a majority.

O'Hara's expression grew momentarily solemn as she continued. "When news of the supposed Communist victory leaked out, demonstrators stormed the Congressional building. Protesters demanded a recount even before the first count was completed. Supporters of communism gathered as well, enthusiastically celebrating their success. Tensions escalated and violence erupted between the two groups. Police were called in, but according to some witnesses, local police were loyal to the Communists and were quick to use force on the anti-Communist protesters to restore order. The President called for martial law, and military forces have squared off against the police with protesters caught in the middle. Some reports indicate protesters have been injured or even killed. Others were arrested and jailed on undisclosed charges. Local news reports out of Prague are that there have been no clashes and the Communist Party has won the majority and assumed power without incident. Steve, you have to wonder about who is filtering the news Czechs are receiving. It varies dramatically from what we are hearing from our correspondents."

Steve Jernigan added a footnote to the story. "According to the local news service in Prague, the police arrested only some criminals who posed a danger to the citizens." He raised one eyebrow as if doubtful of his own words.

The more Nicole watched, the more anxious she became. She paced in front of the television, cracking her knuckles and pausing to pray for her family. She checked her watch for the millionth time. *Are they late? No, not yet. Maybe a little bit, but not really.* She jumped like a startled cat when the door flew open behind her. *Finally!*

Her mom pushed the door shut quickly and slid the deadbolt into place before grabbing her in a fierce bear hug. Adam rushed past them to his room and slammed the door behind him.

"Are you okay? Did you have any trouble getting home? Honey, I was so worried about you coming home all alone when I heard the news." Nicole's ribs screamed and she struggled to breathe, let alone answer the barrage of questions aimed at her.

"Mom, I'm all right. You're hurting me." She winced and pulled away, holding her bruised stomach.

"What's wrong? Nicole, what happened?" Her mother swung her face-to-face, eyes demanding the truth.

"Nothing. Just some kids at school. I'm more worried about this whole election thing. What are we going to do?"

Her mother must be seriously distraught—she allowed Nicole to redirect the conversation instead of pressing her for more information.

"We're going to have to leave, at least for a while. They've started arresting anyone who might oppose the Communist regime: Westerners, Christians, and definitely Americans. The police went to the church an hour ago to question Pastor Michal about us. Pastor Michal didn't tell them anything, and he snuck your father out through some old tunnel or something as soon as they left. He would never tell the police where we live, but they will figure it out soon enough."

Her mother took a deep breath. "Dad is taking the Metro to the airport and will buy our airline tickets and meet us there." She gathered up several of the bags they'd packed this morning. "Hopefully, when this is all straightened out, we can come back for the rest of our things."

Nicole stood in the middle of the kitchen, fists clenched. *No! We can't leave! We need to stay right where we are.* The pain that ripped through her heart hurt more than her bruised ribs. She raged silently against the insanity of it all, but in the end, she had no choice. *Still, why would Communists be concerned about one small missionary family who have seen no more than a handful of converts in five months? It's ridiculous!*

"Mom, this is crazy. Why would they be looking for us? We're just one family. Why would they even care about us?"

Her mother dropped the bags and grabbed her shoulders. Nicole read fear on her face and anger in her voice. "One man is behind all of this. He is the one who gave the order to arrest the demonstrators. He expanded his order within the last hour to include anyone he deems a threat, and he sent the police to the church looking for your father. His name is Vladimir Novak. If the Communists have won the majority, he is the new President of the Senate." She drew in a deep breath and dropped the bomb. "And he is Mara's father."

The words were like another kick to the gut. Nicole had never met Mara's father so she didn't recognize him in front of the Congressional Building earlier. In all these months, she'd never been to their home, never convinced Mara to visit hers. People just didn't invite friends into their house here as they did back home. Even when she heard the man's name on the news, she didn't connect it with her friend whose last name was 'Novakova,' the feminine form of Novak.

"It's all my fault. I gave her the Bible. I talked to her about becoming a Christian."

Now Mara's father's overprotective rage was turned against Nicole's family. The power gained through this election provided the perfect opportunity for revenge. But what would the punishment be?

"Now are you going to take this seriously? Do you understand why I'm concerned?" Her mother's voice rose in pitch and volume. She ran her hand through her hair and took a deep breath. "I am going to put these bags in the car. I want you and Adam ready to go when I come back up to get you, do you understand me?"

Nicole managed to whisper, "Yes, ma'am." She followed her mother to the apartment door, guilt choking any further words.

"Lock the door behind me."

As soon as her mom turned the knob, the door flew open, slamming against the wall and sending them both sprawling. Her mother's head cracked loudly against the TV, knocking it from the cart with a loud crash, and then she lay still.

A giant dressed all in black stepped over the threshold and reached for her mom. Nicole scrambled to her feet, holding her breath. The bald hulk lifted her mother like a rag doll, barely flexing the muscles that threatened to burst though the black shirt. Tossed her over his shoulder. Pivoted back to the entry.

Nicole came alive as her survival instincts kicked her into fight mode. She grabbed her mother's hands where they dangled over his back. "No. *No!*" She shouted as she tried to wrestle her mom's dead weight from his shoulder.

A single shove from his meaty hand sent her stumbling backward.

He spoke in Czech into a mic at his wrist. "Come get the girl."

He continued through the doorway as if headed for an afternoon stroll, only instead of having a tote bag carelessly over his shoulder, he had her mother.

Icy fingers gripped her heart as Nicole struggled to process what had just occurred. His words reverberated in her head: "Come get the girl."

They're coming for me. Who? Why? She didn't know, but they were coming for her. She had to run. To escape as fast as she could.

Adam appeared in the doorway, rubbing his wide, red-rimmed eyes, bag in his hand.

"What's all the noise? Where's Mom?"

"It's going to be okay, I promise. Just come with me right now." Her quavering voice betrayed her own lack of confidence, but she grabbed his free hand before he could put up a fight and ran out the open door. The man in black had taken the stairs across the hall from their apartment, so their only hope lay in the stairs at the opposite end of the hall. *Lord, please let him not send his partner to cover the other end of the building.*

She tried not to drag Adam, but his legs were shorter and he couldn't keep up with her long strides. She fought the urge to yell at him, to berate him for not moving faster, to throw him over her shoulder as the hulk had her mother…as if she even could. Anything to move more quickly.

As they reached the stairwell door, she threw it open and shoved her brother into the darkened recess of the landing.

"I'm going to lock the apartment door. Hopefully that will slow them down. They'll think we're inside and have to break it down to look for us. If I don't come back, go to the church. Don't speak to anyone. Go to Pastor Michal, he'll take care of you."

He nodded as he backed into the corner, clutching the bag which held his prized possessions. "But, Nicole, please come back, okay?"

"Don't worry, I will." Her voice was only a bit less shaky than before.

Sprinting back down the hall, she pulled the string with her key from around her neck as she went. It took less than a second to slide the key in the lock and turn it, but her heart hammered in her ears.

Wait. Not my heartbeat. The sound of boots clomping up the stairs behind me. She snatched the key from the lock and sprinted back down the hall, half expecting to hear the boots following her. As she neared the door, it eased slowly open in front of her.

Panic crushed her as she tried to slow down. Time seemed to wind down to a slow-motion nightmare, her mouth opening in a silent scream. *I was wrong. They've come up these stairs. They already have Adam and now they'll have me as well.* Her heart lurched into her throat.

Until Adam's face peeked through the open doorway! He created a space barely wide enough for her to slip through and then closed the door silently behind her just as its twin at the far end of the hall burst open.

The sound of meaty fists banging on the steel door of the apartment and an angry voice shouting in Czech muffled as they ran down the stairs. When they reached the ground floor, she stopped to listen but heard nothing.

She bent over at the waist, hands on her knees, to catch her breath. "We'll go to meet Dad at the airport."

"But…" Her brother started to argue.

"No, 'buts.' We don't have anywhere else to go." Her voice sounded tight and harsh, even to her. "Just do what I say for once."

"We can't leave Mom!" He protested.

Nicole hesitated. He was right. She had no idea who the man was or where he would take her mother. Torn between protecting her little brother from the danger of these men and protecting him from the truth of what had just happened, she froze.

But what had happened? She didn't know for sure. Her mother's body had been limp, lifeless. Unconscious.

Or worse?

Regardless, she and Adam could not possibly rescue her.

"We have to go meet Dad. Mom wanted us to get away. This is the only way that will happen. And Dad will know what to do." She peeked out the door of the apartment building. A second monster in black leaned against a black Volvo. His back to them, he stood looking up toward the apartment and spoke into a mic on his wrist like the one Baldy had used. She didn't see her mother anywhere. She led her brother carefully out of the building, keeping to the shadows and staying out of sight.

Once around the corner, they hurried to the bus stop. They'd have to take a bus and two trains to reach the airport. *Please, Lord, let Dad be there.*

They reached the bus stop without drawing any attention and stood, waiting anxiously for the next bus. As the bus approached, Nicole saw the black Volvo round the corner. She ducked her head and watched it zip past. She recognized the bald man behind the wheel, but bile rose in her throat when she didn't see her mother.

The number 32 bus pulled up, blocking her view. She and Adam were among the first to board as the doors eased open with a slight hiss. They moved to the back and sat by the rear door where they could exit quickly. When all the passengers were on the bus, it lurched back onto the street, belching black smoke.

Nicole kept her head down and slightly toward her brother to avoid the eyes of the other passengers. The bus pitched roughly as it rounded the corners of narrow streets, winding haltingly toward the city center.

As they approached the next stop, the familiar uniform of a transportation officer stood out amongst those waiting. Periodically, officers would enter the buses, trams, or trains, and randomly check for boarding passes. They had their tickets as always, of course, but what if the transit officials communicated with the police? Were the police looking for her and her brother?

She elbowed Adam and discreetly pointed toward the officer. They stood and edged toward the rear door as the bus slowed down. As soon as the doors opened, they hurried off the bus, moving to the right to avoid the officer. People swarmed all around them, carrying groceries, riding bicycles, and talking on cell phones. They seemed hurried and stressed, rushing about their everyday lives with an unusual sense of urgency. The fear on their faces revealed that news of the coup had spread.

They were not at the right stop to catch the Metro which would connect to another bus line and take them to the airport. There were no signs directing them toward a Metro station, and Nicole did not recall the bus stop at all.

"We need to hang out until the bus leaves, and then wait for the next number 32 to come. Otherwise, we'll never find our way to the airport," she told her brother.

"I know the way from here. Mom and I have been shopping at the potraviny right over there. If we walk about four blocks this way," he pointed down the street to the left as he continued, "there's a tram stop that goes to the Metro."

"Are you sure this is the same one? The streets look the same, and there are as many potravinys here as there are Food Lion's™ back home. They all look the same."

"No, that's the one, I'm sure of it." Adam started down the street, calling over his shoulder, "Come on. Trust me. I know what I'm doing."

Nicole glanced back at the stop where the large red and white vehicle pulled away. The officer had chosen not to get on the bus and stood waiting. Her chances were better with Adam than with the official, so she hurried after her brother.

Her long legs soon caught up to his short ones and she matched her pace to his. Both were silent as they walked past a row of shops and down a side street where walled courtyards guarded large homes. Few shared the sidewalk with them here.

Nicole's pride silenced any acknowledgment that her little brother was right as they emerged from the neighborhood onto another crowded street with a tram stop on the corner. The schedule indicated the trolley should arrive any moment. No one else waited at the stop, and the people on the street hurried by. Some wore concerned frowns, but she detected no obvious signs of the major political shift happening around them.

The summer sun cast long shadows, and her stomach reminded her they had missed dinner. It would be dark before they could reach the airport. The tram arrived within minutes, and they sat in the back and kept their gazes fixed on the floor. Nicole glanced out the window, trying to get her bearings as the tram rumbled down the street. When it rounded the corner and traveled toward the city's center, she recognized some familiar sights.

The evening air had grown cool and smelled of rain as they crossed the street from the tram stop to the Metro station. She grabbed Adam's hand instinctively as they stepped onto the escalator and descended four stories underground. Flat screens mounted at intervals along the wall broadcast news. The din around her drowned out any sound from the TV, but the image spoke for itself. The police wrangled a man to the ground and cuffed his hands behind him, then hauled him upright and swung him to face the camera.

Her father's face stared back at her, frozen on the screen with the caption 'Zatčen!' — 'Arrested!' — emblazoned below.

Nicole nudged Adam then shushed him with a finger to her lips and a quick shake of her head. She leaned close to his tousled hair and whispered, "We can't go to the airport. We'll have to go to the church. Pastor Michal will know what to do." The fear in his eyes made her stomach flip. Suddenly, being the oldest weighed on her shoulders like an overloaded book bag.

The Metro stop brought them a block and a half from the church. They emerged under a street light cycling on as darkness fell. As they climbed the steep street toward the church, the acrid scent of smoke filled the air. The sun had set quickly and the streetlights cast an eerie amber glow as smoke obscured their light. They slowed as she realized the smoke emanated from the church itself.

There were no firefighters and no police on hand, but a large crowd had gathered on the sidewalk in front of the church. As they approached the fringes of the crowd, Nicole caught words and phrases, but the bitter comments made no sense.

"Ona zasloužit ono," one elderly woman said. Nicole translated roughly, "They got what they deserved."

"Tupy!" she caught a grim-faced man muttering under his breath. She rose up on her toes and craned her neck to see through the crowd and barely recognized the outer wooden doors of the courtyard. One hung askew from a single remaining hinge, and both were ablaze. She couldn't see through the crowd and the flames if the fire extended beyond the courtyard to the church itself.

Tears rolled down her face, the salty taste sneaking into her gaping mouth. Tears not only for Pastor Michal and what might have become of him, but also for herself and for Adam, for her parents and for her friend, Mara. *What can we do? Who can we turn to now for help? Adam and I are alone.*

The responsibility of protecting Adam weighed heavy on her. Her breath came in short gasps, and the street around her tilted first one direction and then the other as she wobbled. Her knees turned to Jell-O™ and threatened to give out. Worry and fear overwhelmed her until a mild tug on her arm broke into her shock. Adam led her around the corner into an alley.

"Nicole. Nicole! Snap out of it." He pulled at her hand and snapped his fingers in front of her.

"What are we going to do?" she moaned. "What happened to the church? To Pastor Michal?"

"Listen. I talked to a lady in the crowd. She said the police were looking for Pastor Michal. They broke down the door. But they couldn't find him, and when they left, some people in the crowd went crazy. They trashed the church and then set it on fire."

"So they don't have Pastor Michal? Oh, thank you, Lord." The words escaped like a sigh of relief. "At least he's safe. But now what do we do?" She spoke to herself more than her brother. "Maybe we can go to—"

"'Cole, I think I know where he might be," Adam interrupted. "When I was at the church one day, helping him set up for services, he showed me a room in the cellar. A secret room left over from World War II. He uses it to store books and old furniture. He said during the War they used it to hide people because it has a passage out through a tunnel under the church. The tunnel is from a thousand years ago. Maybe more."

Nicole eyebrows shot up, doubtful of his story.

"Pastor Michal said the passage came out somewhere in this alley. That's how Pastor Michal got Dad out of the church when the police were looking for him." He started walking down the dark alley, dragging her along behind him as he spoke.

"I don't know if I can find it in the dark or not, but there's supposed to be an entrance around here somewhere." She followed in stunned silence as he inspected the walls, searching for the architectural element which marked the entrance to the passage. In the darkness of the lane, she could barely see her hand in front of her face, let alone any sort of detail.

The distant sound of the mob grew louder. Nicole glanced behind them and saw shadows dancing as the crowd approached, carrying makeshift torches. The angry voices echoed between the tall buildings lining the alley. She plastered her back against the rough stone wall and jerked Adam back hard enough to make him yelp in pain. As the crowd passed by, the firelight cavorted through the urban canyon, illuminating the gothic architecture.

"There it is," he whispered. "We should be near the

opening."

"I don't see any door. What are you talking about?" she snapped, cynical about the prospects of a secret room, let alone Adam's ability to find it in the dark.

He slid further down the alleyway, his back against the wall and his fingers gliding along each mortar joint between the old stones. She followed behind him with arms crossed.

"Stop," he whispered. "I found it." His fingers slid into a crevice in the mortar. "Quick! Stand right beside me as close as you can," he whispered.

She closed the space between them and held his right hand tightly, plastering her own back to the wall as well. Adam pressed the fingers of his left hand into the mortar and the barrier behind them gave way with a grinding sound. It slid directly backwards for about two feet to reveal a small space to their left. The narrow gap only allowed them to slide in sideways one by one, and it was pitch dark. Nicole considered the wisdom of entering this crypt, but the noise of the crowd coming closer again frightened her more than the dark. Sometimes there was no good option. No right answer. Just a choice between bad and worse. She held onto her little brother's hand and slid into the murky space. There was no turning back.

Josefov, Prague, Bohemia
June 18, 1577 anno domino
The moon glowed low along the horizon as the three-some scurried through the underbrush along the river bank. Rabbi Judah Loew ben Bezalel gestured to his son-in-law

and his favorite pupil, indicating they had reached the loam pit he sought. They dug into the soft clay, scooping blobs of the grayish matter into a pile and slowly shaping the sticky material. The moon had reached its apex when they stood back and admired their handiwork. The once shapeless clay now lay before them in the form of a man.

The Rabbi handed a tiny scrap of paper containing his incantation for fire to his daughter's husband, Josef ben Ibrahim. "You must walk around the figure seven times as you recite the words," he instructed the young man. Josef flashed a dubious glance at the elder rabbi but nevertheless obeyed. As he paced around the body of clay, it began to glow a brazen orange. He stopped in his tracks, but the rabbi urged him on.

Next, the Rabbi handed a similar scrap to his pupil, Elisha ben Benyamin. The youngster was barely past his bar mitzvah and his hands trembled as he followed the elder's example. Tracing Josef's steps, his voice a mere whisper, he recited the Rabbi's words for water. The red-hot clay cooled and grew moist, sending plumes of steam into the air. The boy finished his seventh round and collapsed on the ground. Josef knelt beside him, trying to comfort himself as much as to console the boy.

The Rabbi stepped forward and placed the tiny scroll containing the name of Yahweh into the mouth of his creation. His eyes darted to Josef whose face reflected his own excitement and terror. He took one step and then another, reciting the words from the Mishnah.

"And the Lord God formed man of the dust of the ground, and breathed into his nostrils the breath of life, and man became a living soul." The last word echoed in the dark

night even as the creature's eyes opened. They had passed the point of no return.

Chapter Seven

Underground

Nicole felt the stone door slide shut behind her, cutting off all light. She tried to turn toward Adam but banged her shoulder on the opposite wall of the passageway.

She slid her hand into her pocket and retrieved her cell phone. The glow from the screen gave her a moment of sheer joy before the spinning wheel of death reminded her she hadn't charged it last night. The glow faded as quickly as it had sprung to life.

"You have to slide along sideways, 'Cole," her brother whispered.

"Did Pastor Michal show you this passageway, too?"

"No, actually, he only showed me the entrance through the basement, but he told me about it. He said it's narrow so you can't tell from inside the building there is any space here. But you have to slide along and be careful because it has steps." She heard his feet stumble and his hand tugged at hers as he found the first step. The thought of falling and being trapped in the narrow space, unable to get up, made her cling to his hand and try to brace herself against the wall in front of her with her free hand.

"Thanks, that was close," Adam said.

"Be careful! I think I should lead."

"Well, great. Go ahead. Oh! That's right…you can't get past me." She didn't have to see his expression to recognize the sarcasm in his voice. "So I guess you're going to have to trust me or go back. And since I don't know how to open the passage from the inside…"

"I guess you're right. But be careful, okay?"

"Duh. I don't want to fall either, ya' know." Step by step, inch by inch, they descended far below the buildings above. The concrete wall behind her back grew rougher, and the smell of mildew overwhelmed her as the air grew cool and damp. She imagined she could make out some shape or light, but there was none. It seemed like hours since they slipped through the doorway, and her legs began to ache from the strain of edging along the corridor.

A noise beside her ear gave only an instant's warning before something crawled into her hair. She let out a piercing scream and released Adam's hand to beat blindly at the creature. Instinctively, she jerked forward, slamming her forehead into the opposite wall. Stars danced in the dark as she fought to keep from sinking to the floor by bracing her hands on the wall. Whatever had crawled into her hair had fled in terror and was forgotten amid the blinding pain. Adam slapped at her in the darkness as he tried to regain her hand. Tears mingled with the blood which trickled from her forehead down the side of her nose and tasted salty and metallic as she tried to suck in the musty air.

"What happened? Are you all right?" His voice sounded small and frightened.

Nicole fought to catch her breath and calm down. Even in her agony, she had to keep her head together to get them out of this tomb.

"I'm all right. Something scared me and I hit my head, but I'm still here." She pulled the bottom of her shirt up to wipe the blood from her forehead and the tears from her eyes. Adam had finally connected with her elbow and held on as if it were a lifeline. She pried his fingers loose and held his hand.

"It's going to be all right. Adam, don't worry, we're going to be fine. Let's keep moving. There has to be an end somewhere." Her voice sounded less certain and she hoped he didn't notice.

She heard a muffled sniff before he replied, "I'm fine."

They continued the slow, steady pace downward. The steps gradually became less distinct until they were sidestepping down a shallow, uneven slope. The jagged walls were no longer those carved by man but the natural formation of a cavern. At intermittent points, the cave widened enough to turn and walk forward rather than sideways, but the gloom slowed their progress with the constant need to feel their way.

"Stop a minute," Adam said, as he halted and she bumped into him. "I think I hear something."

Nicole strained to hear any sound. She wondered if she imagined it, but she did hear something. A crackling …no, a trickling! It sounded like water running in the distance.

"Keep going, maybe we're near the end." She urged her little brother on. The path twisted and slowed their progress further as they edged around each curve. She kept hold of his hand with her left hand and kept her right hand up in front of her face, protecting her injured head from any unexpected outcrop of rock. She lost count of how often her hand struck a rough protrusion and she had to duck her head to get through the space.

The path widened, and she stumbled into Adam's back again when he came to an abrupt stop.

"Whoa. Why did you stop?"

"I'm trying to find the right tunnel. Pastor Michal said there was a place where the tunnel split, but he didn't tell me which one to take."

"I'm sure he didn't think you'd actually be using the tunnel." Her fingers blindly explored around the edges of the cavern until she found two openings. One was a narrow crevice barely wide enough for one person. The other felt wider, but was only as tall as her shoulder.

"I'd rather have to duck my head than be squished like that again."

Nicole hunched over to keep from hitting her head and entered the shorter passage. They shuffled along the uneven ground, and still the passage grew smaller. She pulled on Adam's hand.

"I have to stop a minute. I can't keep going, bent over like this." She longed to stand up and stretch out her aching back muscles, but there was no room.

"Maybe we should crawl on our hands and knees," said Adam.

"Anything is better than this, but I won't be able to hold your hand. I can't see a thing. What if we get separated?" The only thing worse than being in this place would be if she were here alone. Gratitude for her brother's presence washed over her like a tidal wave. *That was weird.* She shook it off.

"I've got it!" he said. "I'll get on my hands and knees, and you put your hands on my ankles. So when I move one leg forward, you'll move your hand forward. Kind of like the elephants in the circus."

"Only you could make this sound fun." Nicole laughed. She heard Adam getting down on his knees in front of her and kneeled down, patting the damp ground with her hand until she found his tennis shoes. She grasped his bony ankles, and said, "I'm ready, let's do the elephant walk."

As they crawled slowly forward, the floor of the cave continued to slope downward and the moisture on the ground soon soaked through the knees of her jeans. They crept along for what seemed like hours as Adam led the way.

As the ground became wetter, it also grew slippery and, without the traction of their shoes, their hands and knees slid along the slimy surface. Rivulets swirled around her. The ice cold water numbed her fingers, knees and toes. The trickle grew deeper with each bit of progress they made. One moment the water tugged at her fingertips where they grasped her brother's ankles, the next moment it shoved her knees forward like a bully, knocking her off balance.

The stream pushed her along and she couldn't stop. She let go of his ankle with one hand to try to grab hold of something...anything. But her dead fingers barely sensed the rough walls as she sped by. Adam slid down the path ahead of her, rushed along head-first by the natural spring of water as she followed close behind, holding one of his ankles. She prayed they wouldn't slam into the rocks as they picked up speed. Her fingers slithered around his ankles and she tried to keep them locked tight and still keep her knees under her so she wouldn't be face down in the water. They glided faster and faster down the natural waterslide in the dark, with no idea what waited at the end of the ride.

Adam's voice echoed back to her.

"WHOOOOOAAAA! I can't stop!" Adam yelled. And then, "I see a light!"

Nicole saw it too. They raced toward an opening filled with an eerie white light.

They exploded into an open chamber, blinded by the sudden bright light, and splashed into a pool of icy water. Her fingers were still clenched around his feet as they sank deep into the pool. Her mind reeled from the shock. *Let go. You have to let go or you won't be able to swim.* A voice of reason intruded on her muddled thoughts. She dodged Adam's wildly kicking legs and pulled through the water. Her face broke the surface, gasping for air.

Slowly, her vision adjusted to the change from darkness to light. She tread water as she scanned the pool for Adam. His head appeared and then submerged, then bobbed up a second time. He knew how to swim, but the shock of the cold water must have taken his breath away. As he went down for the third time, she grabbed the back of his shirt and pulled him to her. His body was limp and lifeless. Wrapping one arm over his shoulder and across his chest, she struggled to the side. The edge of the underground pool dropped off steeply and she wrestled to push his dead weight onto the ledge before climbing out with trembling arms.

She knelt over him, panting from the effort. His face was ashen, blue veins standing out against the pale white of his closed eyelids, and her stomach tightened. She rotated his head to the side and pressed both hands forcefully into his abdomen. Water gushed from his mouth and nose. He sputtered and coughed, but he was alive. She bowed her head to his chest and pulled him close to her, praising God. Her tears mingled with the water from the pool as her ragged breathing began to slow.

A sound drew her attention away from her brother. She glanced up and realized for the first time they were not alone.

CHAPTER EIGHT

Familiar Faces

Nicole gaped at the dozen or so faces circling her and her brother. There were some children, but most were adults ranging from a little older than her to one or two gray-haired senior citizens. She tried to read their expressions, but the bluish glow of the fluorescent camp lanterns cast eerie shadows, transforming their features into a grim nightmare. The harsh light made Adam's face a ghastly pale and his purple lips trembled slightly from the cold and shock as she hovered over him. The curtain of strangers finally parted and a friendly face emerged.

"Pastor Michal!" She jumped to her feet and ran to the elderly man. Her brother struggled to his feet, his body shaking violently, and followed closely behind her.

"Nicola! Adam! How did you find us? I've been so worried about you since I learned your parents had been captured." The clergyman hugged them close despite their soggy clothes.

"Pastor Michal, I f-followed the p-passage, the one you told me about!" Adam said through chattering teeth.

"But you must have taken the wrong fork in the path …the other passage brings you into this cavern without quite such a splash."

"I'm not sure I'd call it a passage, more like a crack in the wall." Her head still throbbed and she gingerly touched the large knot on her forehead.

"Oh, my goodness, look at your head! Come, come, and let us take a look at that, my dear."

The fatherly figure led her and Adam to an area where a stack of blankets covered the stone floor. A petite woman in scrubs knelt beside a young man with one leg contorted at an impossible angle. Nicole's stomach rose in her throat at the sight as two large men held the injured man still while she pulled on his foot to straighten the leg. He let out a shriek of pain before losing consciousness. She watched, feeling a little woozy, as the woman splinted the fracture before she grasped his ankle, searching for a pulse. Finally, the doctor dug in a first aid kit for some medicine and gave directions for his care in Czech to one of her assistants as she handed him the bottle.

She twisted to face them, dragging her hand across her forehead and tucking an errant lock of blond hair back into her pony tail.

Pastor Michal made a quick introduction in English, "Dr. Ruzicka, this is Nicola and her brother, Adam. As you can see, she's had a bad knock on the head."

"How did this happen?" With the doctor's strong Czech accent, Nicole barely recognized the words.

She told the embarrassing story of the spider scaring her into whacking her head on the wall of the cave.

"Well, you have a little laceration, but it doesn't look as if it is very deep."

The doctor pulled a small flashlight from her pocket and used it to examine the wound.

"I do not think you will need stitches."

Next, she flashed it in each of Nicole's eyes.

"And I don't see any sign of concussion. So we clean it up, give it some antiseptic, and use an ice pack for the swelling, and in a few days, you'll be as good as new."

Nicole listened carefully, trying to translate the woman's heavily-accented English into something she could understand and praised God she wouldn't need stitches. After seeing the young man's broken leg set without benefit of anesthetic, the thought of having the wound stitched made her stomach flip. She sat on the damp floor of the cave and allowed the doctor to clean and dress the wound from her small first aid kit. The doctor snapped the ice pack and shook it up to activate it before pressing it to her forehead.

"Now, hold this on your head until it's not cold anymore."

"B-but I'm s-soaking w-wet," Nicole protested as her teeth chattered from the combination of the wet clothes, the cool, damp air, and the ice pack. Dr. Ruzicka glanced from her to her brother, who stood nearby, arms crossed, shivering, and dripping ice water.

"We must get them some dry clothes or they will develop hypothermia. Pastor," she said, turning to the clergyman. "Do we have any extra clothes? Or towels? Something dry and warm."

Nicole wished she had grabbed her bag before they escaped the apartment, but there had been no time. She wasn't sure where Adam's bag had been lost, but if he had somehow managed to keep hold of it through their trek, the cans of food tucked in the top of the bag had taken it straight to the bottom of the pool.

"I will ask. Perhaps someone can help us." She watched as the pastor shuffled quickly amongst the people huddled around each lantern. He came back shortly, leading a short, squat woman who held out a set of clothes for each of them with a perplexed look.

"Praise God, children, these clothes are a gift from Him."

"What do you mean?" Nicole said.

The pastor explained, "I asked everyone, 'Do you have any clothes? Were you able to bring anything extra?' and each one said, 'No, we have only the clothes on our backs.' Then this woman said, 'Here, these are for the children,' and she handed them to me. She said a man stopped her and gave her these clothes. She was scared and didn't want to cause a scene, so she took them. She didn't know why he gave them to her because she has no children. She said the man told her, 'These are for the children.'"

The woman's head bobbed in agreement as he spoke, and she pressed the clothes into their hands and smiled, revealing a shortage of teeth. "Děti, děti."

She and Adam looked at one another in stunned silence. They took turns and changed into the dry clothes while the pastor and the doctor held up a blanket for privacy.

Her teeth had stopped chattering, and she settled onto the blankets with the ice pack on her forehead. Her eyelids drooped, just for a moment, as she reveled in the feeling of warm, dry clothes and the security of being surrounded by the love of God. The stress of hiding, of running, of knowing her parents had been arrested…all the fear dissolved. Her eyes flickered once or twice, long enough to see Adam following Pastor Michal as the shepherd moved among his sheep, offering prayer and words of encouragement. *Always seeking to protect and guard us. What a heavy burden he bears.* Fear and adversity brought home the real meaning of 'shepherd' in a way she'd never really considered.

Josefov, Prague, Bohemia
January 18, 1578 anno domino
Six months had passed since the evening along the riverbank when the Rabbi brought his creature to life. For six months, the clay-man had inhabited his cellar, serving his creator faithfully. Calling his handiwork Josef, Rabbi Ben Leow directed the being about various tasks around his home and the synagogue — except on the Sabbath, when he removed the tablet from Josef's mouth and he, like the entire community, observed a day of rest.

The Rabbi's students had kept their silence, albeit primarily for fear of being thought mad, but nevertheless, the truth about the Golem remained a secret. Those who saw him serving in the Rabbi's household or at the synagogue were simply told he was a distant cousin, mute, whom the Rabbi had agreed to provide for in exchange for his service. Rabbi

Ben Loew had sent the Golem out into the city only twice and only at night. Both errands had been successful.

Still, the creature's growth remained a source of concern. He brushed the thought aside and focused on the issue at hand. The Rabbi eased his wrinkled frame down the earthen steps into the darkness. A groan from below acknowledged his approach. This evening's errand was the most critical. The emperor Rudolph II had responded well to the first two visits. But, as of late, the attacks on their community had increased once again.

The emperor needed some more encouragement.

Nicole awoke with a start, uncertain of her surroundings and imagining monsters lurking in the shadows. Sitting up, she tried to get her bearings. The cave was dark, with all but one lantern extinguished. A small group sat in a circle under the lone source of light while the other inhabitants of the cave were curled in small piles here and there, trying to sleep. To her left, she saw a mother sitting with her back against the rough wall of the cave, her head hanging on her chest as two small children dozed with their heads in her lap, her arms curled protectively over them. Her heart ached for her own mother, and she wished it could be her and her brother curled with their heads in her mother's lap.

Next to the woman, she could barely see the form of a man on his knees. His hands covered his face, and he murmured a prayer as he rocked slightly, back and forth. The cave was too dim for her to see much further, and to her right, the icy pool confined them. The cave seemed to be a long, narrow space which stretched down the length of the pool. On the far side of the water, the cave rose straight from the water, curving inward to form the ceiling of the cavern.

Pastor Michal glanced her way and came to kneel beside her. "Are you feeling better?" he asked as he gently lifted the ice pack and checked the abrasion on her forehead.

"Yes. My head still hurts, but at least I got some rest," she answered. Her lips felt thick and slow and her throat dry and scratchy.

He fetched a small bottle of water for her and helped her sit up to sip it.

"How is it you have bottled water down here?"

"When I first came to this church, I heard stories from some of the oldest members that the church had once been used to help Jews escape the Nazis during World War II. I searched through the journals of previous pastors until I found notes — very cryptic. It took me years of studying them and searching the church until I found the entry to the secret room where they would hide them below the church's cellar and then use these tunnels to help them find their way to freedom. God impressed on me through His Word that we might one day find use for it once again, so I began to collect and store items we might need. Blankets, bottled water, first aid kit…we have at least some meager supplies to help us."

"Where did all these people come from? How did they get down here?" They couldn't have all come the way she and Adam had.

"They are church members — or friends and family of church members. They were in the church for a prayer meeting for the election when the news came. Others, like the man you saw with the broken leg, came to the church seeking sanctuary after being attacked. When the police came, I asked Jakub to bring everyone to the secret room to hide."

"Jakub? Are you sure you can trust him?"

The pastor seemed surprised by her question. "Nicola, we must not judge by our sight but with our heart and the Spirit of God."

He continued his story. "First, the police were asking about your parents, and then they began questioning me. They left to find your parents but said they would return and expect answers. We had only moments to gather supplies from the church and lead the people through the storage room to the cave before the crowd outside broke in. I could hear them upstairs in the sanctuary. They were bent on destruction." Tears hung on his lashes and he brushed them away. "And then I smelled smoke."

"The doors to the courtyard were burning, but I don't know if they burned the whole church or not."

After a long pause, he continued. "I called your father to warn him just before we left the secret room. We are safe here, but we have insufficient provisions for the people. If we are not able to leave, we will not survive long."

"We saw on the news that the police arrested my father. Some men took Mom. Pastor Michal, when they took her she hit her head. I don't know…" She couldn't bring herself to voice her fear.

The pastor shook his head silently. "As a young boy, we heard stories of people who would disappear.

My father said the Communists would take them away because they were troublemakers. Then one day, his brother disappeared." He pursed his lips and looked away. "The man who was attacked said he saw the news of your father. He will be arrested and charged with espionage. I am so sorry, dear one."

"What? Charged with spying?" If it weren't so frightening, it might have been funny. "My parents are not spies. That is ridiculous."

"Of course not, dear. This is a ruse, a trumped up charge, in order to justify the actions of this new 'government.' They will charge anyone who opposes them with spying, rush through a sham of a trial in secrecy, and execute them. It is as it once was. We are all criminals once again."

Nicole broke down in tears, overwhelmed by the gravity of her situation. "But how…how can they do this?" Her shoulders shook with each sob that welled up within her.

Pastor Michal sighed deeply. "In the old days, before the wall came down, they would accuse people of spying. They would fabricate evidence against them or twist the truth. The news mentioned they had seized your father's computer and they are searching the hard drive for evidence. They will create files and make it appear your father sent information to the American CIA."

"But there has to be a way to prove they're innocent! There has to be something I can do. I can't let them…" She couldn't force the words out of her mouth, couldn't allow herself to think about what he suggested.

"I am sure your parents are most concerned with the welfare of you and your brother. They would not want to put you in danger. You must stay here, where we are safe, and we must pray for your parents. They are in God's hands now, as always." He patted her shoulder in a gesture she supposed was intended to comfort her. After a few minutes, he rose slowly and returned to the small group around the lantern.

Nicole sat crying and tried to get control of her fear. She sniffed and wiped her face on the sleeve of her shirt as her mind raced through a thousand different plots to rescue her parents. She dreamed of storming the city jail in Hollywood fashion and breaking them out in a blaze of glory. She imagined calling the American government to send the U.S. Army storming in to oust this insane regime. She even envisioned the rapture occurring this very moment and her parents disappearing before an unbelieving jailer's eyes!

But each plot fell flat in the face of the current reality. She was a fifteen-year-old girl in a country where she barely spoke the language and was a fugitive. She curled into a tight ball on her side as silent tears ran down her face and puddled in the palm where her cheek rested.

Adam came over and touched her shoulder gently. "'Cole, are you asleep?" he whispered.

She sniffled. "No, leave me alone."

"C'mon, I've got an idea. An idea about Mom and Dad."

She rolled toward her little brother. "What kind of idea?" she asked as she wiped the tears away again. *Am I seriously considering taking advice from my little brother?*

"You remember a couple of months ago when we got a virus on the computer and it destroyed everything?"

"Yeah, what does that have to do with anything?" She could feel the irritation welling up inside her and took a deep breath to summon patience.

"Well, Dad didn't want it to happen again, so he signed up with this service, a backup service. You know, they automatically backup all the information on your computer each time you log on to the web."

Nicole caught the idea. "If I could get a copy of the last backup before they were arrested, it would prove they are innocent." She propped herself up on her elbow and considered how she might actually pull this off.

"I would have to get the information to the news media. It would have to be very public in order to keep the government from destroying the evidence. But how do I get the backup?" She wasn't asking the question, just thinking out loud.

"Dad said if the computer got messed up again, we could call and have the backup company send us a disk with the files, but that would take too long. He said we could also go on the internet and download the files to a flash drive, then upload that to our computer or to a new computer if ours had died."

"Great. Well, I don't think we have internet or a computer down here so what good is that?"

"All we have to do is go to one of those internet cafés—" Adam's voice rose with excitement and several people glanced their way. She cut him off.

"*Shh!* Whoa, there, little man. Who said anything about going anywhere? I've got to figure out a way to get that information from here. I can't take a chance on us getting caught." She straightened up and crossed her legs in front of her on the blanket. "Do you know the name of the company? Or a phone number, anything?"

"All you have to do is get to a computer that has internet, then login to the website with the password. It's easy, I watched Dad do it," the boy insisted.

"Do you see a computer down here? Do you see a network cable? Anyone using WiFi?" Her voice rose sharply and she pushed aside the pang of guilt that rose with it. "How on earth can we get on the internet from down here?" Then she recalled Pastor Michal's words. He had been able to use his phone in the secret room below the church. She snapped her fingers and jumped to her feet, making her head ache again.

Adam tagged along behind her as she approached the pastor.

"Pastor Michal, I have an idea of how we can free my parents." She pulled him away from the others and whispered her plan. "If we can use my smartphone to get on the internet, we can send my dad's backup computer files to the media…they will prove Dad isn't a spy."

"Someone may be watching the church. We would risk them finding all of us." The old man appeared to be weighing the consequences, but in her mind there was no choice but to take the chance. The doctor she had seen hours before approached the pastor and pulled him away to speak to him about her patient, and that seemed to be the end of the discussion.

"What are we going to do, 'Cole?" Adam stood at her side, looking up at her, his eyes wide with expectation. She had an idea, but her conscience battled over dueling priorities. She couldn't let her parents be killed, but she also didn't want to be responsible for the lives of the believers hiding in this cave. In the end, she would have to take the risk.

"Did you see where they put our clothes?"

Adam seemed unsure but answered, "Over there." He pointed to a pile of soggy clothes lying on the ground near where she had slept.

Nicole glanced over her shoulder to where the pastor stood with the doctor, listening intently to her report. He would never notice, she told herself. She could get to the secret room, make contact, and send the information before he even noticed she was missing. No one would see her because she'd only go as far as the secret room.

She slipped over to the pile of clothes and dug her cell phone out of the wet jeans and slid it casually into her pocket. Adam was right beside her again. "What are you doing?" he whispered urgently.

She glanced from side to side, "I'm going to try to save Mom and Dad. Now, how do I get out since I can't go back the way we came?"

He grinned. "We'll have to wait until Pastor Michal comes over to this side of the cave. We can move over to the other side now that you're okay, and when he gets busy, I'll show you the way through the church."

"You aren't going anywhere. And I'm not going

through the church…it's all burned, remember? I'm just going to the secret room. I'll connect to the internet and send the information to the news and then be right back."

"I'm going too! You can't find your way without me. And if you leave me here, I'll tell Pastor Michal where you've gone. Besides, I know the password for the backup service and you don't."

She pulled back her fist and wanted to punch him in the arm when she saw Pastor Michal turn toward them. She put her arm around Adam's shoulders instead, squeezing him until he squeaked as she smiled at the elderly gentleman.

The pastor checked her forehead once more. Seeming satisfied that the bump on the head wasn't serious, he returned to the subject of her parents.

"Nicola, I understand you want to help your parents. But we can't put everyone in danger. Let me speak to some of the others. Perhaps we can find a way to help your parents."

She forced a smile and nodded as if she understood. She and Adam rose and ambled over to the other side of the cave as if they were mingling with the others. Nicole picked up an unused lantern, and they eased into the shadows until they found a natural crevice in the wall.

"I can't risk anything happening to you. You need to stay here, and you need to give me the website and password so I can do this."

"No, I'm going with you. Besides, you don't know how to get into the room in the church."

"And you do?" She tried not to draw attention to

their squabbling, but her voice rose sharply turning a few heads in their direction.

"Yes, I asked Pastor Michal about how they all got down here and he told me about it."

She had to concede the point. "All right, you can come. But be quiet. I don't want anyone to notice we're gone."

Adam took the lead, feeling his way along a narrow path once again. When Nicole thought the light from the lantern wouldn't be seen from the cave, she flipped it on and they proceeded silently until they came to a dead end. They were surrounded by solid rock. The only option was to go back.

"Great, Einstein. Now what?" She bit her tongue but not soon enough. And she wasn't quite repentant enough to apologize.

"Just a minute. The door is here somewhere." Adam pushed and prodded at each lump and bump on the rock until one finally gave way. As the rock shifted, it swung to the right and opened into the secret room below the church. Although it smelled of burnt wood and water dripped through the planks in the ceiling, it had been saved from the fire.

They froze for a moment, listening for any sound from the cave, and then shoved the large rock back into place. The interior face of the hand-hewn rock was finished to match the rest of the walls. The room contained neat stacks of books and old furniture covered with sheets, all of it now soaking wet. Apparently, at some point, the firefighters had arrived and extinguished the blaze above, leaving behind a soggy mess.

Nicole pulled the cell phone from her pocket and

pressed the power button. Nothing. She shook it and tried again.

"It's wet. You need to put it in rice to dry it out."

"Really? Really? Adam, do you see any rice here?"

She slid the back of the phone open and took out the SIM card and wiped it on her shirt. She used a corner of her shirt to dry the inside of the phone and replaced the card. Pressing the power button again, it finally powered up slowly. One bar of service. How had Pastor Michal made a call from this room? She held the phone up and began moving around the room, watching for any sign of network coverage. It was no use. They were still too far below ground to pick up the nearest signal.

"We're going to have to try to get upstairs to the church."

Adam strode toward the opposite wall and twisted the doorknob. It didn't budge. He pressed again, this time leaning his body weight in as he pressed. Still, there was no movement.

"Maybe something is blocking it from the other side." Nicole began to lose hope. "What are we gonna do now?" she said in exasperation as she twirled and leaned on the door with her arms folded in front of her. As soon as her weight hit the door, the locking mechanism released and the door swung open. She fell to the floor at the bottom of the narrow steps leading up to the sanctuary.

"You found it!" Adam cheered. "Way to go!" She took hold of his hand and pulled herself up.

"Thanks, but I don't think I had anything to do with it." They crept up the stone stairs, emerging in the room behind the altar which contained the steps down into the baptismal pool. Nicole peeked out into the sanctuary, horrified to see the destruction caused by the mob. The fire left the pungent scent of smoke trapped in the wood and fabric of the old sanctuary, and the pews were overturned, the altar table up-ended, and the pulpit knocked to the floor. She fought back tears.

"Whoa," Adam said in a flat, lifeless voice. "What a mess."

"We'd better get this done and get out of here or we're gonna get caught before we even have a chance to help Mom and Dad." She pulled out the phone again, thrilled to see a strong signal. Then the phone beeped once and shut down, the battery completely dead. "What are we going to do now?" She leaned against an overturned pew and let the tears fall.

"We can't give up, 'Cole. I know where we can get on the internet."

"Where?" She folded her arms and sniffed.

"It was outside the Vysehrad metro station. There's an internet café there on the corner." His smug grin widened, but Nicole could have kissed him.

"Vysehrad is only two stops from here." She weighed the danger of venturing out against the con-sequences of doing nothing. It didn't take long. "I'll have to risk it. Tell me exactly what you remember af-ter you got off the metro."

"No way. You're not going without me. I know how to get there and you don't. And I speak Czech bet-ter than you do."

She hated to admit he was right, but she hesitated.

If both of them disappeared, what would Pastor Michal think?

The sound of footsteps approaching made the decision for her. She grabbed Adam's hand, holding a finger to her lips to silence him, and dragged him down the side aisle and behind a pew as a tall figure entered through the vestibule.

She watched from the shadows as Jakub entered the sanctuary and stood surveying the damage. He squatted amid the ashes and flung burnt and charred pieces of wood to the side, searching, but for what? He stood abruptly and strode toward the center aisle. When he had nearly reached the pulpit and paused with his back to them, she nodded to Adam and the two slid silently out of the church. As they emerged into the courtyard outside the church, the early morning sunlight blinded them momentarily. Nicole peered carefully out of the wreckage that remained of the courtyard doors onto the usually busy street. Deserted. And the rare people she saw walked with heads down, grimly seeking their destination.

"Wait, I have an idea," Adam whispered and pulled her back into the courtyard.

She listened to his plan and reluctantly agreed. With Jakub now nowhere in sight, they crept back into the sanctuary and smeared the damp soot on their face and clothes. Within moments, they looked like homeless waifs who had spent their lives on the tough streets of the city.

As they stepped out of the courtyard onto the street, the hair on the back of her neck prickled and she glanced behind them. No one. She shook off the sense of foreboding.

They walked to the metro station, trying to mimic a casual shuffle. Once on the train, they sat in a corner together and stared out the window, avoiding eye contact with anyone else on the train. As the doors were about to close, a last minute traveler rushed in. He ran breathlessly into the car, came directly toward them, and sat down across from them.

"Where do you two think you are going?" he asked.

CHAPTER NINE

An Unexpected Ally

Nicole stared into the dark eyes of Jakub. Despite seeing him weekly at the church, she was held captive by his intent gaze as he spoke to her for the first time. He repeated his question. "Where do you think you are going?"

"We…we're just…" Her lips seemed too thick to form the words.

"We're going to prove our parents aren't spies!" Adam jumped in.

She rolled her eyes and glared at her brother. "Shh! We can't trust anybody."

"You can trust me," Jakub's English was better than she expected, but his expressions sounded formal and stiff. His deep baritone evoked strength and security. "Pastor Michal asked me to follow you. I was supposed to keep you from leaving, but you slipped out before I could stop you. I will help you, but we must be careful. The police are looking for you. They will use you against your parents, if they can."

She hesitated a moment, but she had nothing more to lose. He had already discovered them, and maybe he could help them. She looked at Adam and he nodded. She shrugged and gave in. "How can you help us?"

"I don't know. What is your plan?"

Moments later, huddled in a corner of the train with her brother and Jakub, they reviewed their plan. Jakub seemed skeptical. It was weak. She would go to the internet café, log on to the internet and the site which held their backup, and send a copy of the backup to the media to prove her parents had not been spying.

As the train approached the station, the trio meandered to the nearest door. Jakub led the way, scanning the platform for uniforms before leading the other two through the station. A beeping sound drew her attention to the flat screen broadcasting news to those waiting on the platform. She gasped as she recognized her own face gazing back at her from above a scrolling alert. She tugged at Jakub's sleeve and jerked her head toward the video alert.

"They're looking for me." She revised her statement as she saw her brother's face replace hers on the newsfeed. "For us."

"The internet cafe will be streaming news. They will certainly recognize you or your brother. But I can go and send your father's computer backing up."

Adam chuckled at his statement, but she was unconvinced. "What if the owner realizes you're helping us? He could turn you in."

"No, he is a friend. He will not turn me in. But he doesn't know you. You, he would turn in. I can do this, please." His dark eyes pleaded, and Nicole studied the platform, uncomfortable under his relentless attention. Her head bobbed in silent agreement.

They took the escalator to the surface and started down the sidewalk, conspicuous on the empty streets. *Where are all the crowds?* Heads down, they walked up the steep, narrow thoroughfare.

Nicole stole a glance at their new-found collaborator. His stride was longer than hers as he stood at least a foot taller. She and Adam struggled to keep up. Dark hair hung over his ears and collar in an amateurish cut. It looked good on him though. His eyes, she knew already, were so dark a brown they were just this side of black. He moved with his head down and his hands deep in the pockets of faded jeans. He glanced back and forth, up and down the street, and he remained a pace or two in front of them. With a few words, he'd taken charge of their mission. She fought off the irritation of having her authority usurped and reminded herself he was there to help them.

They covered the distance from the metro station to the internet cafe in ten minutes, but the tension made each second last forever. As they approached the corner, Jakub stopped short and turned to them.

"Wait. You stay here." His urgent whisper did not allow for argument as he grabbed their arms and directed them into a narrow alley between two buildings. Before Nicole could protest, he was gone. She fought the urge to follow him, knowing her foolish pride could put them all in danger. One look at Adam and her heart lurched. The smudges of soot from the burned out church stood out against his pale skin, and his blue eyes were round pools of fear.

She pulled him close and hugged him. He didn't resist her affection as he normally would but held on tight. Which was more surprising—her sudden need to comfort him or his eager willingness to accept it? She wasn't sure.

Her voice sounded foreign even to her. "It's going to be okay. Don't worry, he'll get the information and Mom and Dad will be fine." The words reassured her brother more than they did her. She pushed aside the image of her mother's limp body hanging over the shoulder of the man in black.

The two leaned against the wall and waited. *What if Jakub doesn't return? What if he was wrong and the owners of the cafe did turn him in? What if the police are two steps ahead of us, waiting inside to capture us? What if...*the possibilities for failure multiplied until her head swam. Tears welled up, and she tried to blink them back before Adam saw, but it was too late.

"Don't cry, 'Cole." The boy who had seemed on the verge of tears himself a moment ago was gone. His voice sounded strong and steady now. He lifted his face toward the sky. "Lord, I pray for 'Cole that you would help her not to be afraid. I know you can help her, because you helped me and I'm not scared anymore."

Fear drained from her body like water down a drain. The hurricane of possible scenarios faded and a warm rush of calm, as if she had entered the eye of the storm, replaced the chaos. The sun peeked over the roof and into the alley, bright as a spotlight on her face. The tears streaming down her face were ones of peace and joy.

"Thank you, Adam, your faith and your prayers have such power." Her voice broke. "What would I have done without you?" It was her turn to hug him and not let go.

"Psst, I have it. Let's go." Jakub had reappeared at the entrance to the alley.

She glanced away and brushed the tears quickly from her cheeks so he wouldn't see them.

"You got it!" squealed Adam.

"Did they give you any trouble? What happened?" whispered Nicole. "I thought you were going to send it to the news stations."

Jakub pulled a flash drive from his pocket. "I got it on this so you would have a copy. No need to make copies, we can use electronic mail to send it to the news stations. They were talking about your parents when I came in… they had seen on the news that they were spies. The government issued a, what you call? A curfew? A police officer came in just as I had saved it. I didn't have time to send it to anyone yet."

"So how do we get it to the news media?" She took the small piece in her hand and flipped it over. She recalled the news story she had seen the day before. "Even if we get it to them, I'm not sure it will do any good. They are not reporting the truth. They're reporting whatever Novak tells them to report."

"What if we sent it to someone else? Someone outside of Prague who could make sure it went to the President or something?"

Nicole started to roll her eyes at Adam's suggestion, but then it sparked an idea.

"Adam! You gave me a great idea. If I can get it to

my online friends—to the International Mission Force—they could send it to news stations outside of the Czech Republic. Maybe that would keep them from hurting Mom and Dad if the whole world was watching."

Jakub smiled. "We find another cybercafé and send these files to them in less than five minutes." He started to step out of the alley onto the street but jumped back, colliding with Nicole who stepped back onto Adam's foot. Adam squealed and grabbed his foot, but Jakub quickly covered his mouth.

"The policeman who was in the shop is coming up the street," he hissed.

The three hurried to the far end of the alley, glancing up and down the street. Just as they emerged, Nicole glanced back to see the officer. Worse. He saw her. He spoke into a mic at his wrist and ran into the alley.

"Run!" she yelled and grabbed Adam's hand instinctively. They were running uphill, the street guarded on both sides by four-story buildings fused together, doors closed. No place to hide. The cobblestone road made a hairpin turn and the buildings gave way to walled homes, their courtyards covered in ivy. An ancient brick wall rose on the left, covered with ivy as well, and the cobblestones seemed to come to an end in front of a large opening in the brick. Shored up by heavy columns, the tunnel supported a road which ran along the top of the brick wall.

As they emerged on the other side into a wooded park, barred windows peered down from a room of some sort over the tunnel. Perhaps the wall served as an ancient fortification and the tunnel a gate onto the grounds, guarded at one point in history from the garrison above. Nicole only had a moment of curiosity before Jakub pulled them behind a row of shrubs which bordered the brick wall. The three huddled near the ground, panting, watching as the police officer emerged from the tunnel. He continued running a hundred feet or more before slowing and surveying the area.

"No. I don't see them anywhere." His words carried across the wooded grounds as he barked into the mic. He threw his hands in the air and stomped back toward the bridge.

Nicole held her breath as the cop stopped just even with the gap between wall and hedge. A glance in their direction and he would see them.

"I'll keep looking until I find them, sir. Yes, sir." The man continued walking, disappearing under the bridge.

Her breath escaped in a long sigh, but her heart still pounded.

"We need a new plan," she whispered in case the cop doubled back.

"It's not safe for us to stay here. We need a place to hide." Adam was still out of breath.

"I know a place not too far from here. Follow me." Jakub led them along the brick wall and through the woods not far from the cobblestone lane which wound through the grounds of Vysehrad. They climbed the steep street until they reached the Leopold Gate, approaching the ancient castle fortress.

Her legs burned from the climb, and her heart

pounded as she tried to keep up. A quick glance behind her told her Adam was out of breath again as well. Finally, Jakub led them behind the small, round, stone chapel, hidden from the path. Nicole and her brother collapsed in the shaded grass to rest and catch their breath from the strenuous hike.

"We will wait inside until it is dark," Jakub said quietly as he waited for the other two to stop panting.

"How can we wait?" She gasped for another breath of air. "Every moment we wait they have my parents locked up. Every moment"—Nicole took a deep breath and revealed the fear driving her on—"could be their last!"

"You cannot help them if you are locked up as well. When it gets dark, we can travel more safely. Until then, we can hide in the tunnels underneath the chapel."

She sighed in consternation. Nicole could see his resolve and knew he would not be swayed. And since she wasn't sure where to go, she was powerless to proceed without him.

He put a finger to his lips and held up his palm to tell them to stay put while he peered around the side of the round stone building. He waved for them to join him as he approached the door.

The chapel consisted of a round turret of stone, with a second significantly smaller turret budding off the side, a cupola emerging from the center of the larger one, and each adorned with one small, arched window. The only entrance was through an ancient wooden door hinged with elaborate iron fastenings, arched as well, and framed with a broad façade inscribed in Czech: Sancte Martine Ora P Nob. Nicole watched as Jakub used a slim blade to open the ancient lock and swung the door open enough to allow them in.

"What kind of church is this?" Adam asked their young tour guide.

"It is an old chapel, the oldest building in Prague, actually. It was built around 1100 AD. Up until recently, no one knew it contained a secret underground passage." He grinned as he pulled the old door closed and walked to a section of the floor near the small window. He stomped on the floor near the wall, and a single floorboard tipped upward just as he stooped to grab it with one hand. He knelt to reach under the board next to it, releasing a catch which opened a trap door and revealed a stone staircase. The trio descended carefully into the basement, following the path of light created by the small window. When they reached the bottom of the stairs, he lit a torch which hung on the wall and closed the door to seal them in to wait until evening.

Lifting the torch from the wall, he led the siblings through a narrow passage to a huge room surrounded by statues. "These are the original statues from Karlov Most, Charles Bridge. This room is called 'Gorlice,' and it is where the armies would gather and where they would store their weapons." He hung the torch in a sconce at the wall as the three sat in the circle of light to wait.

"You seem to know all about this place," Nicole commented.

He seemed surprised by her compliment and glanced away as if embarrassed.

"So what else can you tell us about?" Adam asked eagerly.

"Well, you know we are at Vysehrad — which some legends say was the first castle in Prague. There is little of the castle left, only a wall of the fortification overlooking the river. The legend says Princess Libuše stood on the hill at Vysehrad and prophesied that a great city whose fame would reach to the stars would one day stand where Prague stands today."

"Princess Li-boo-shay? I've never heard of her." Nicole tried to copy his smooth pronunciation.

"We learned about her this year in school." Adam was obviously thrilled he knew something his sister did not. "She was the daughter of King Krok. They call her the Mother of the Czech Nation." He took a deep breath and launched into his version of Czech history. "So the king had three daughters, no sons, and she was the youngest. They all had special powers. The oldest one, Kazi, was a healer, and the middle sister, Teta, was a sorceress. But Libuše was supposed to be the wisest and she could see the future. So the king wanted her to be queen when he died.

But there was a man who tried to steal another man's land and when the case came before her and she decided against the thief, he told them they were all weak for letting a woman rule over them and they should have a king like all the other nations did. Libuše waited but not one single person spoke up for her. She prayed about it and then announced she would get married. So she put clothes for a prince on the back of her horse and told her servants to follow the horse and they would find the man she would marry. The horse led them to a farmer who was plowing named Přemysl and he became the king." He paused for a breath.

"You learned all that in school?" Jakub's voice sounded almost envious. He continued where Adam had left off. "Some believe that Libuše's castle, Libušin, was located here on the grounds of Vysehrad. There are ruins on the cliff overlooking the river known as Libuše's bath, but they are actually the ruins of a watchtower. While Libuše ruled, women were given rights and treated well, especially compared to other countries during the seventh and eighth centuries. But when she died, the men ridiculed all those who listened to her wise counsel and because of their disrespect, many of the women fled or fought back. There was war between the men and the women, known as the Maiden War."

"Wow, a war between men and women." Nicole shuddered at the thought of such a battle.

"Of course, the men won." Adam grinned and it irritated her to see Jakub smiling as well.

"Hmph. Let's change the subject before there is a new 'Maiden War.' This one might not turn out as well for either of you." She surveyed the musty room. "Tell us about some of these statues."

"These used to be on the Charles Bridge, but they've been replaced by replicas or statues that are more popular now. Uh, let's see." He rose and walked slowly around the hall carrying the lamp to illuminate the stone sculptures. "This is King Wenceslas with his grandmother, St. Ludmila. There is a Christmas song that mentions him: 'Good King Wenceslas looked out on the feast of Stephen, when the snow lay round about, deep and crisp and even...'" Nicole smiled at the deep tone of his voice. "As the song goes, he was famous for his generosity and kindness to the poor, even the Roma."

He ducked his head as if he hadn't meant to include that last piece of information. A moment of awkward silence followed before Adam jumped back in.

"Pastor Michal told me that he was a Christian who died for his faith. His father was a Christian but his mom was a pagan priestess name Drahomira. His father died when he was young and his mother took over and wanted him to be a pagan too. He was raised by his dad's mother. She was also a Christian. But Drahomira had his grandmother murdered and tried to win Wenceslas back, but he already knew the truth. When he was only eighteen, he got a bunch of people who were loyal to the faith and overthrew his mother. But his younger brother was raised by his mother, and the two of them planned to kill him. His brother stabbed him to death on the steps of his brother's chapel."

"I thought Wenceslas became the Holy Roman Emperor Charles IV, the one who the Bridge is named for." Nicole tried to demonstrate that she had learned something during her time in Prague.

"People often get them confused. This Wenceslas lived in the tenth century. Charles IV, who was born Wenceslas or 'Vaclav' in Czech, was born about four hundred years later."

"You know an awful lot about history…" She realized the insult hidden in her words too late.

"For a Gypsy?" There was a slight edge to his voice as he spat out the slur. "You learned in school, but Roma children have to go to special schools and are taught very little. I love to read and study. Many Romani do, but it is not always encouraged in our culture. My father disapproves of me spending time reading. He also disapproves of the time I spend with Pastor Michal, but that is another story."

Nicole tried to change the subject, feeling guilty for her prejudice. "What about this statue?" She pointed out one of a horse appearing to leap with a rider on his back. Unlike most statues on horseback, the rider was not a soldier or knight but looked like a barefoot peasant.

"Ah! Horymír and Šemík! According to legend, during the reign of prince Křesomysl, the prince was so obsessed with riches that he encouraged all the Czechs to search for gold and silver he believed was buried in the ground."

"Buried here?" Adam's eyes were wide with excitement.

"Perhaps. But Horymír was a farmer who warned that if the farmers all spent their time foolishly searching for treasure instead of farming, there would be a famine and the people would starve. But those searching for gold did not listen and they became so angry at him, they burned down his village. He and his followers retaliated by burning down the village of the miners, but when the King heard about it, he had Horymír thrown in prison and sentenced to death. They asked him for his last request before his execution and he pleaded for one last ride around the yard on his beloved horse, Šemík."

"Why would they let him do that? Wouldn't he just escape?" Nicole ran her hand along the flank of the bronze horse, mesmerized by the story.

"They did not think so because they were on the top of a cliff. Escape seemed impossible. But when he climbed on the horse's back, he whispered something in Šemík's ear and the horse leaped off the cliff, slid down, and swam across the Vltava, saving his master's life."

"What a great story!" Adam had apparently not heard this one.

"That isn't the end," he continued. "Šemík lay injured and dying, but before he died, the legend says he spoke to Horymír in the voice of a man and asked him to build a tomb for him. No one knows what became of the tomb, but it is said that Šemík sleeps within the rock at Vysehrad, waiting another opportunity to help when all is lost."

Nicole settled onto the floor, hugging her knees to her chest as Jakub continued with strange tales woven throughout the history of the country. Sitting in the gloom of the Gorlice added an air of mystery to the political intrigues and miraculous events that comprised Prague's history. Their current troubles were momentarily lost, and her head sank onto her knees as she drifted into a land of dreams filled with treasures, miracles and monsters.

Karlov Most, Prague, Bohemia
January 31, 1578 anno domino
The Rabbi and his minion waited in the shadows cast by the statues which guarded Charles Bridge – Karlov Most. He had received word that the Emperor had ridden out this evening, according to his custom, to escape the castle and ride his stallion along the banks of the river. He would have to pass this very spot to return to the castle.

Ben Loew shivered in the cool moist air rising from the Vltava. Snow blanketed the landscape and continued to fall, hiding the footprints they'd left just an hour before. This would be his most daring move yet. Josef's past visits to the Emperor had been effective only to a point. Lacking the power of speech, the hulking figure had terrified the young Emperor but had not been able to demand relief for God's children. Tonight would be different. The Rabbi would make it clear that the golem answered to him and any more attacks on the Jewish quarter of the city would be met with resolve by their protector.

The distant clatter of hooves brought his attention back to the need at hand. He signaled to Josef to wait until the rider approached them before emerging from the shadows. His servant obeyed faithfully. At the last possible moment, Ben Loew gave the command and Josef stepped in front of the galloping horse, hands raised, and emitted a low guttural sound which was his only means of communication.

The horse reared and let out a frightened whinny, and his rider lost his hold and tumbled to the cobblestones with a thud. His mount snorted and raced off in the direction he'd come, away from the hulking monster.

The Rabbi hurried from the shadows and helped the

Emperor to his feet, but the man fell to his knees once more when he saw Josef towering over him, larger than the statues which lined the bridge. Rudolf covered his face with one hand, cowering in fear. "What do you want from me?"

"We want only what all men want — freedom and peace! You must demand justice for the crimes committed against God's people. You must not allow this persecution to continue." *The Rabbi's deep voice boomed through the quiet night and Rudolf bowed his head to the cobblestones at the sound.*

"I have no control over them! The people do not listen to me," *he whined.*

"Silence!" *The Rabbi commanded now and the Emperor obeyed.* "You must find a way to make them listen. You are the Emperor!" *He nodded to Josef who lifted the king to his feet.* "Go now and return to the castle — do not speak of what you have seen, but take swift action to bring these men to justice who dared attack Yahweh's children."

The Emperor's knees seemed to buckle for a moment when the golem released him, but as the Rabbi watched, Rudolf ran, trembling, across the bridge to the castle.

CHAPTER TEN

No Way Out

Nicole awoke to Jakub shaking her shoulder and declaring it was evening. She wasn't sure when she had nodded off but she would have to avoid listening to his tales before napping. She shivered and rubbed her eyes as if she could erase the images that haunted her dreams.

"So, we need to find a place where we can get on the internet and send those files. But you said yourself the news about my parents is out. Any place that has internet access is also going to be looking for us because they've seen the story in the news. We could send it from my phone, but it's not charged, and I left my charger in the apartment. Do you know where we could get a charger? And we need do it quickly and then get back to the church before the curfew."

"I know a shop that sells them near Old Town, but we shouldn't use the Metro."

"But Old Town must be miles from here."

"Only a couple of kilometers. It's almost dark so we should not be seen."

They crept out of their hiding place and down the

steep steps along the cliff overlooking the Vltava River. As the glow of the fading sun dimmed, they reached the bottom with Nicole and Adam breathless and lagging. A tunnel through the mountain seemed the perfect moment to catch their breath without fear of being seen, but Jakub didn't slow down.

Emerging from the tunnel, she glanced back at Vysehrad towering on the cliffs behind them. The blackened twin turrets of the medieval cathedral stood in stark relief against the crimson sky as the sun sank below the roofline across the river. She stretched her neck to ease the tension there and realized they would hit Old Town within the hour if they could keep up the pace Jakub set. Her legs pumped as fast as she could move them but were no match for Jakub's long strides.

"Wait...wait! Jakub, we've got to rest!" Nicole huffed and puffed while she clasped both hands over the stitch in her side. The bruise on her stomach ached and her head throbbed.

Jakub steered them both out of sight into an alley and allowed them to catch their breath. Adam bent over at the waist, hands on his knees, taking in long, deep breaths as the color of his face faded from hot pink to a more natural shade. She leaned against the side of the building with her eyes closed as she willed herself to breathe slowly in and out. *Slow down,* she commanded her heart, but it refused to obey. *Great, Nicole. Way to impress the guy with your inability to walk half a mile without dying. Breathe in, breathe out. Breathe in...*

With her breathing almost back to normal, she opened her eyes to find him peeking from their hiding place.

"I don't think anyone saw us," he said over his shoulder.

Adam straightened and faced Jakub, his fists planted on his waist in defiance.

"C'mon, you gotta give us a break. We can't keep up with you!" His voice carried a hint of whining that drove her crazy, but Jakub didn't seem to notice.

"I'm sorry. I forget sometimes that my legs are long and you Americans only walk to your cars." Jakub faced them with a grin.

The smile did not soften the insult, and Nicole bristled. "Well, before we start sprinting again, are you sure this shop will be open?"

"They are always open. They are open for the tourist and even the Communists do not want to hurt the tourism. When we reach the place, I will go in. You wait outside."

She wanted to argue, but she knew it was their only hope. With their pictures on the news, she and her brother were bound to be recognized.

"But if you are seen with us, then you could be caught. We may even get caught before we get to the store." Adam jumped in.

Nicole nodded. "We're putting you in danger just walking down the street with you, not to mention putting our parents' rescue at risk."

Silence enveloped them as they considered how to deliver the files while protecting Jakub and the mission.

"You and your brother go back to St. Martin's Rotunda. Go there and wait. Once I send the files, I will come find you there." Jakub spoke as if the decision was made and stepped toward the street, but she grabbed his arm.

"Wait a minute. What if something happens to you? Or what if we get caught? I don't think we should split up." She resented him taking control of the situation and refused to trust him completely with their success or failure. And she wasn't about to admit she couldn't possibly make it all the way back up the stairs along the cliff in the dark.

He shook his head slowly. "If I get caught—if I don't return by midnight, go back to the church. No one will recognize you in the dark, but you must not take the buses or metro. They will be looking for you. Believe me, we will all be much safer this way," Jakub argued, but she would not be persuaded.

"What if we followed behind you at a distance? It wouldn't look like we're together, but if we're caught, you would know it. And if anything happens to you, we'd know it."

Jakub cast a glance at Adam and shook his head again. "Is she always this difficult?"

"You have no idea," Adam answered.

Jakub admitted defeat and headed north toward Old Town. She waited until Jakub reached the next street and then sent her little brother out. She paused again to allow him a head start and then set out after them. She kept her distance from Adam but also kept Jakub in view.

The streets grew more crowded as they approached the busy tourist section in the heart of the old city, although the political upheaval had reduced the usual mobs. Nicole's view of Jakub was interrupted by turns in the narrow streets and the crowd, and she worried about the distance between herself and her little brother. With a dozen people between them, she lost sight of him and her heart leapt in her throat. Her legs burned as she closed the distance until she was within reach of him.

She glanced up in time to see Jakub under the orange glow of the streetlamp as he rounded the corner toward Old Town Square. They were blocks from Karlov Most and winding through the streets which had led people toward the city's center for nearly a thousand years. The street-front shops were an odd mix of ancient architecture and modern materialism, selling everything from jewelry and crystal to souvenirs and magazines. Nicole kept her focus straight ahead and ignored the calls of shopkeepers looking for a sale.

They took a right down another tight lane and the crowds increased as they approached the Prague Astronomical Clock. It was one of her favorite places to visit in Prague, and she knew it must be drawing near the hour as people gathered in the square. As the clock struck the hour, small figures representing the twelve apostles paraded out of one door and back in another as a skeleton representing death rang in the hour. The clock had kept time accurately for over six centuries, even surviving the destruction at the end of World War II of the Town Hall building on which it was mounted. It not only kept the hour and minute, but the month and day, phases of the moon, and the astrological signs of the zodiac. She loved to stand among the tourists and hear English, Spanish, and Italian, even

Chinese. But seldom would she hear any Czech spoken. For the natives of Prague, the amazing clock had become mundane.

Her musing ended abruptly as a pair of uniformed officers strolled into view across the street not ten feet away. Nicole faced the shops and pretended to admire a garnet necklace. She watched the soldiers carefully in the reflection on the glass. When they moved on down the street and she breathed a sigh of relief, she turned to look for Adam but he had disappeared in the crowd of people.

Panic surged through her as a thousand fears assaulted her. What if the police grabbed him? Or worse, she knew enough about the darker side of Prague to know there were those who bought and sold children for purposes too grim to contemplate. She rushed up the street, peeking into each shop. Finally, she reached the small store front that advertised 'Cell Phone Chargers.' Peering through the plate glass window, she spied Jakub at the counter, handing the clerk several bills for the small charger. But Adam was nowhere in sight.

She stood on tiptoes, looking up and down the street. *Where could he have gone? I only took my eyes off of him for a moment!* As she scanned the crowds, she spotted the police officers elbowing through the crowds in her direction. One raised a cell phone to his ear as they dodged the tourists.

Nicole spun and ran up the street, darting between people and looking for Adam all the while. A glance over her shoulder confirmed the officers were definitely pursuing her. She turned the next corner and recognized the gelato shop they visited often. As always, crowds pressed into the small space from before lunch time until midnight.

"Excuse me," she murmured in Czech as she pushed her way through the line of people waiting to order the rich gelato. She headed toward the back, then peeked back through the crowd to see her pursuers standing outside, looking up the street. They'd soon realize she had entered the shop. She continued through the kitchen, ignoring the angry shouts of the owner as she passed through.

Pushing open the back door, she emerged in a dirty alley lit by a single streetlamp at the far end. To her right, a refrigerated box truck blocked the end of the alley. Hearing a commotion from inside the shop, Nicole veered to her left and sprinted up the alley.

Just as she realized the commotion must be the police pushing through the crowd in the shop, two soldiers rounded the corner under the amber light and raced up the alley toward her. She stopped her headlong flight and reversed direction, nearly falling on her face in the process.

The police had not yet made it through the shop, and, from the sounds coming from the back room, were being assaulted by the owner. Nicole had nowhere to go. The only door led back into the shop. The soldiers ran toward her, shouting in Czech for her to halt. As they came, one reached over his shoulder and pulled a large black weapon into firing position. *There's no escape.* She backed slowly away from the soldiers as they closed the distance. Tears streamed down her face. *I'm caught. Adam is lost. What if Jakub is caught as well?*

Her back struck the delivery truck and a tide of fear overwhelmed her. She covered her face with trembling hands and began to pray out loud, "Oh Lord, how can this be happening? Help me! I'm trapped! Lord, there's no way out!" Evil was closing in all around her.

Prague Castle, Bohemia
February 8, 1578 anno domino

Emperor Rudolf remained sequestered in the Castle, afraid to ride out alone despite the fact he had heeded the Rabbi's warning. He had ordered his soldiers to leave the residents of Jewishtown alone and had decreed anyone caught in that area of the city who didn't belong there would be punished by death.

A rap on the door gave notice that Von Rumpf had returned from delivering his decree. He beckoned his chamberlain forward and the man approached in a halting gait, his clothes disheveled and his face bruised.

"Good heavens, man, what do you mean, appearing before me in such a state?" The emperor waved his perfumed kerchief under his nose to mask the scent of blood and manure emanating from Von Rumpf.

"Your Excellency, the people are rioting in the streets because of the Jews! They are demanding you take action against them, drive them from our land for the safety of your people. They beat me as a warning – a warning to His Excellency of what they will do if you fail to act boldly."

Rudolf rose in anger. "I will not be threatened! I am the Emperor and they answer to me. I do not answer to them."

He clapped his hands sharply and called to his Master-at-Arms, who appeared in the doorway.

"Send your soldiers into the town at once. Bring back one of the townspeople who are rioting...and one of the Jews as well! I will make an example of these two for both the townspeople and that Rabbi. They will learn who is the Emperor and they will not soon forget.""

The Master-at-Arms vanished on his mission.

"You..." The Emperor waved in disgust at Von Rumpf, "Leave my presence until you are presentable and never enter my courts again in such a state or you will find yourself in worse condition than you are already."

Von Rumpf limped away.

The Master-at-Arms and his guards returned to the castle with two townspeople in tow, one a young ruffian they had caught among the rioters and the other an elderly Jewish woman unable to move quickly enough to escape when they rode through Jewishtown.

The Emperor felt a prickle of concern for the old woman, which only made him all the more determined to squelch the compassion he saw as weakness.

"Very well done," he nodded at the Master-at-Arms. "See that they are thrown to Mohamed for his evening meal."

CHAPTER ELEVEN

Divine Intervention

Nicole felt the hot breath of her adversary about to devour her. The prayer was still on her lips when strong hands clamped onto her elbows and lifted her into the air. It barely registered she had landed on her bottom in the truck before the door slammed shut, extinguishing the amber light of the city lamps. She heard two loud thumps and then the truck jerked forward, sending her sprawling. The muffled voices of the officers shouting for the driver to halt went unheeded.

With the door shut, the cargo area of the delivery truck turned pitch black. She searched desperately for a glimpse of her rescuer, but it was impossible. The hair on her neck rose. *Is this a rescue or a kidnapping?* Her desperation to find Adam turned to fear for herself. But as the van picked up speed and careened through the narrow roadways, her hero clicked on a small flashlight and revealed himself. It was Jakub.

"What? How on earth...?" Nicole stammered. Then a thought occurred to her. "Did you get the charger?"

"Yes, I have it." He pulled the small package from his pocket.

"How did you know I was trapped? How did you find me?"

"I saw you peek in the window. Then I saw the police following you. I knew you would not be able to outrun them. I followed them, and when they went into Cream and Dream, I knew you must have gone inside. There was nowhere else for you to hide," Jakub explained. "I came to the back door. The owner is a friend. I told him to delay them as long as possible."

Questions swirled in her mind, but she tried to stay focused on essentials. "Okay, so, who is driving this truck and where are they taking us?"

"It is the delivery driver. He has another delivery to pick up and then he will take us back to the church. We can trust him."

"Another delivery?" Nicole thought their safety should come before any pickup he might need to make, but didn't want to complain so soon after being rescued.

The chilly air in the refrigerated truck made her teeth chatter. Jakub shone the flashlight on the spot beside him where he leaned against the side of the truck. "Come sit over here. You won't slide around so much and it will be warmer."

She scooted over to sit between Jakub and a crate filled with cartons of heavy cream. "You haven't asked about Adam." Her voice sounded small and flat, even to her own ears. "I lost him. I glanced away for a moment, and he was gone. Did you see him?"

"Don't worry about your little brother. He is

smart. He will think of something." Nicole stiffened at his lack of concern. *How can he be so heartless?* She pulled her knees up against her chest and wrapped her arms around them. Each turn of the truck caused them both to sway from side to side as they tried to maintain balance.

"Do you think they will follow us?" she said quietly.

"They were on foot, but they may call in others. We must be sure we aren't being followed before we make our pick-up."

Nicole wondered again about the pick-up. *What on earth could they need so badly as to risk being caught?* She tried rocking back and forth and thinking about something else to keep warm, but her teeth still chattered in the cold.

Jakub reached his arm around her shoulders and pulled her closer without a word. She hesitated for a moment before accepting the warmth. He seemed completely unaffected by the cold, and his strong arm provided an anchor to keep her steady.

They shifted one way and then the other as the truck seemed to be negotiating a maze. She passed the awkward moments by praying silently for her brother and her parents. She had finally stopped shaking when the truck lurched to a stop. The two waited quietly until the rear door clanged open. The driver looked like Jakub, but older, with a mustache and dark hair peppered with gray. He spoke sharply to Jakub in a language Nicole didn't recognize and disappeared into a dilapidated apartment building.

A moment later, he returned, and she gasped

when she saw Adam with him. He gave the boy a boost into the back of the truck and then jerked the door shut without another word. Nicole scrambled toward her brother in the dark, grabbed him, and hugged him tight.

"Are you okay? How did you get here? I took my eyes off you for a minute and you were gone!"

"I'm fine. When I saw those two cops, I went into the shop and Jakub's friend brought me here to hide," Adam answered.

Nicole spun on Jakub like a feral cat. "Why didn't you tell me he was safe? How could you let me worry like that? I thought he was lost and it was my fault!" She slapped at him, knocking the flashlight out of his hands. It cut off the instant it hit the floor, leaving them in the dark again.

Jakub grabbed her hands, easily stopping her assault. "I left him with my friend, but I did not know if they had been captured. I did not want to give you false hope."

Relief over Adam's safety deflated her anger a little. She tried to pull her hands from his strong grip.

The truck rounded a curve and Nicole lost her balance and fell hard into Jakub. The two of them rolled on the floor as the truck took another hard turn and they were hopelessly tangled. Thankful for the darkness which hid her blush, she tried again to get loose. Jakub let go of her hands and helped her back into position against the wall. In a moment, he had found the flashlight and clicked it back on.

Once they were situated again, she searched for a way to break the uncomfortable silence. "So, is the driver your father? He looks just like you."

"Yes, I'm sorry if he seemed angry. He is upset with me for getting him involved."

"It's me who should be apologizing. You and your father have risked everything to help us. I don't know where we'd be without you. Thank you, and tell your father thank you for us too." She reached her hand out to her brother who was barely visible within the circle of light provided by the flashlight. "Adam, are you all right? I was worried about you."

"I'm fine." He scooted a little closer and grabbed her hand. "I was worried about you, too."

They huddled quietly in the cold as the truck swayed through the winding streets of the city. The silence was finally broken by Nicole's stomach letting out a ferocious growl to remind her it had been almost a day since they'd eaten.

"Don't worry, we will be there soon. We should have something to eat." Jakub didn't elaborate on what that might be, and she didn't particularly care.

The truck finally squealed to a stop and they all fell forward. The door swung open as they tried to sit up and the orange glow of a streetlight momentarily blinded her. Jakub's father motioned sharply to leave the vehicle, and Jakub led them down a steep cement stairway at the back of an abandoned warehouse. He jiggled the doorknob several times before the latch released and the door opened slowly from within.

The dim light from the street revealed a small group huddled around a table. They looked like refugees from some sad commercial for a charity, their dirty faces and unkempt hair revealing a desperation she knew her own appearance mirrored. She turned to Jakub and whispered earnestly, "I thought we were returning to the church."

"We can't risk it now, not with…" His voice trailed off for a second before shaking his head as if coming to his senses. "We will have to wait until we are sure we haven't been followed. You will be safe here until I come back. I'll go and bring something to eat"—he glanced at the eager faces looking his way at the mention of food—"for everyone."

Nicole's stomach seemed to growl in support of Jakub bringing sustenance. "That sounds good. Why don't you give me the charger, and I'll get my phone charged and send the files while you're gone?"

Jakub gave a quick snort and shook his head. "It won't do any good. There is no power here."

He slipped back out the door and left her and Adam to meet their companions. As the two of them introduced themselves in Czech and explained what had brought them here, the dirty faces broke into tentative smiles. Nicole's hands shook as she sat in the metal folding chair offered by an elderly man with wiry white hair squashed by a floppy, worn cap.

She listened as each one shared their story. They had been run out of one abandoned building after another. Some had lost family members over the past winter due to exposure after being evicted from a building in better condition than this one they now called home. These were Jakub's friends and family. They weren't simply hiding in the warehouse temporarily, they lived here. With each frightening tale, a stronger bond grew between them. They were just like her, trying to survive in a society where underlying prejudices had suddenly exploded to the surface in hate and violence. Some had survived brutal attacks by mobs of people. Within moments, they had forged a bond of common suffering stronger than any friendship.

"Would you mind if I pray for you and your family?" Nicole directed her question to the man in the cap who seemed to be the patriarch of the clan. He met her gaze with curiosity and shrugged. When Jakub returned, Nicole prayed for each of them, for the loved ones they had mentioned, and for those who had abused them. She closed the prayer with thanksgiving for God's provision of food and quickly opened the bags Jakub deposited on the table. A loaf of bread, cold cuts, a cucumber, and a tomato. A feast to her hungry gaze. They worked together, using the older gentleman's pocket knife, to quickly slice the vegetables, bread, and cold cuts, and served them with tepid water from the rusty faucet in the corner of the cellar. Nicole could not think of a time when she had enjoyed a meal so much.

The amount of food Jakub brought had seemed not nearly enough for the entire clan. But as she finished her sandwich, plenty remained on the table. She peered around and her companions were hungrily devouring their food. Each came back for a second sandwich. She didn't even scold Adam when he went back for thirds. Still, there was food left. When they finished the meal, Nicole took a moment to pray again, praising God for the miracle they had witnessed. She heard their voices joining in, and while she could not understand their words, their genuine gratitude showed in the tears rolling down dirt-stained faces.

Jakub carefully wrapped up the remaining food and returned it to the canvas bags. "We'll take it back to the cave. I don't think Pastor Michal had much food left there."

His father grabbed his arm and pulled him into the shadowy corner of the cellar. Their voices carried easily, reverberating around the concrete walls, but she had no idea what they were saying. His father finally threw his hands in the air as if Jakub were simply beyond reason. The teen shrugged and walked to the door, waving them over to follow.

"He refuses to drive us to the church. We'll have to walk." The anger in Jakub's voice masked the hurt in his eyes. She winced at the tension and the knowledge that she and Adam were the source.

"Maybe you could tell us how to get to the church from here. You've done so much for us." She glanced at Jakub's father. "I don't want your father to be angry with you for helping us."

He shook his head and opened the door. "We will go up the stairs, and then turn right at the end of the alley. Try to stay out of the light from the streetlamps."

She stayed close to Adam and eyed their surroundings, surprised to find that after all their driving, they were near where she had been rescued that afternoon. A curfew had been issued, so they traveled in the shadows through the narrow alleys around Old Town Square.

Jakub led them alongside St. Nicholas' church.

The amber lights shining on the church illuminated the baroque details of the jade twin turrets and allowed the small band of travelers to hide in the shadows of the recesses below. Without warning, Jakub disappeared around a corner and the Nicole and Adam were left alone in the dark.

CHAPTER TWELVE

Follow the Leader

Nicole froze, her heart pounding as she scanned the shadows for Jakub. Panic began to seize hold of her when he emerged from a hidden door in the side of the column. The ornate structure of the building and the angle of the lights conspired to keep the doorway a secret. Jakub motioned for her and Adam to join him in the darkness. A burst of white illuminated his face as he gestured for them to follow him with the flashlight.

Creeping down the narrow stone steps, she followed the flickering glow until they emerged in a wine cellar. *A wine cellar in a church? Ah, of course, it must be used for storing the wine for the Hussite church's Eucharist services.* Jakub approached one of the racks full of dusty bottles and grasped a bottle by the neck. As he twisted it in his hand, the rack swung open, revealing a round, brick tunnel in the dancing light. The tunnel was about six feet in diameter. Jakub had to duck his head in order to enter. When the three were gathered inside, Jakub pulled the rack closed behind them. A metallic click indicated it was secured again.

"Wait a minute." Nicole grabbed Jakub's arm.

"What are we doing down here? And how did you even know this place existed?" She had no desire to re-live her most recent underground adventure.

"These tunnels lead all over the city. We can use them to return to the church. I know them all because I've lived here my whole life. Let's just say there have been some times when knowing how to get from one place to another without being followed is helpful."

Jakub spun without another word and led them down the dark tunnel. Nicole stayed close behind him and clung to Adam's hand to keep him at her side. Jakub's tall frame hunched slightly as he focused the flashlight out ahead of the group. The skittering, scratching noises coming from beyond the circle of light sent a shiver up her spine. The tunnel reeked of mold, mildew, and sewage.

"Where are we?" she whispered to Jakub.

"These tunnels were created nearly a thousand years ago. They began as cellars people dug during medieval times to store food and wine. But as Bohemia came under attack from other nations, the people began digging tunnels to connect their cellars so they could escape an attack. The tunnels also served to drain water out of the city into the Vltava River."

"Hence the lovely smell." She wrinkled her nose.

Jakub continued describing the history of the tunnels. "The city would often flood and homes and businesses would be under water up to the second level. The ground floor eventually became their cellars. Over the centuries, they were fortified with brick but had fallen into disuse until the Nazi occupation of Praha. Under the communists, they were sometimes used by the secret police. Some people even believe Hitler hid stolen historical artifacts in these tunnels somewhere. But they've never been found."

"Wouldn't someone have found them by now if they were down here?" Adam's eyes were wide and he hung on every word.

"These tunnels wind all over the city. Or maybe I should say 'under the city'. There are hundreds of dead ends, places where they once led to a cellar but the passage from the cellar to the house has been blocked or collapsed. A person could easily get lost in them, never to find their way out. Although some are accessible as a tourist attraction under Vysehrad, there are miles of tunnels that have never been explored or mapped." They paused for a moment as the tunnel branched in three directions.

"So there could still be treasure down here?"

She knew immediately what Adam had in mind. "But we aren't going to worry about buried treasure right now, are we Adam?" she said in her most persuasive voice.

"I know. We have more important things to worry about, but when we have Mom and Dad back and everything is back to normal, I'm coming down here to look for it." Nicole wondered at him giving in so easily, and she fought the temptation to launch into a lecture about how unsafe that would be. She settled for the fact that he would not go wandering off right now.

"Jakub, not that I don't trust you, but do you know your way around here? I mean, I really don't want to get lost down here." A spider brushed her hand as she rested it on the curved brick wall of the tunnel and she jumped away from the wall. "This place gives me the creeps."

Jakub took her hand. "Don't worry. I know exactly where we are going."

The motley group continued on in silence. Nicole could walk upright comfortably without hitting her head, but Jakub had to walk with his head hunched over. She mentally kept track of each turn, still a little fearful of becoming lost in the labyrinth. Her own muscles ached from tension and from the endless walking she had done during the day. She loved to stroll the streets of Prague, but not at the pace of to-day's trek. Jakub paused for a moment and squatted down to stretch his neck and shoulders.

A trickle of water running through the tunnel made the footing slippery. At times, as they passed under storm drains, Nicole could hear rain falling and noticed the trickle seemed to be growing. Several times, she had slipped and barely managed to keep from falling in the foul runoff.

She steadied herself against the curved wall, resting her bruised and bandaged forehead on her hand as she prayed for the strength to go on. A small, warm hand on her back startled her until she heard Adam's voice join her own whispered prayer. Forty-eight hours ago, they had been bickering over the computer and now, they were a team, united in their faith and in their mission. As they finished praying, she pulled him close and hugged him tight. He ducked his head, obviously embarrassed, and pulled out of her arms to speak to Jakub.

"How much further is it to the church?"

"Not far. We are almost there."

"But we still haven't charged my phone and we still haven't sent the files to prove Mom and Dad are innocent." Nicole wondered if they had accomplished anything at all besides spending the day hiking through the city and evading the police.

"Don't worry."

Jakub set out again. With renewed energy, she lifted her chin and followed him. On the streets of Prague, the trip might have taken forty-five minutes, twenty if they took the Metro. But following the underground passageways took nearly two hours from the time they slipped into the church in Old Town until Jakub pushed open a heavy metal blast door and they found themselves in one of the Metro tunnels.

Jakub leaned forward and looked both ways for trains and then knelt to put his hand on one of the rails. He stood up and faced Nicole and Adam.

"This part is tricky. We have only a short time to make it from this entrance to the station and to climb up onto the platform before a train comes. You also must be careful not to touch the rails."

"But you just touched it." Adam argued.

"Yes, the one rail is safe, but it is better to not touch any since you don't know which one is safe and which is not. We will wait until the train goes by and then go right behind it. That will give us the most time."

They waited behind the heavy door, listening for the sound of the train approaching.

"So, why does this tunnel connect to the Metro?"

Jakub laughed. "It is part of the old Ochranny System Metro…the Metro Protection System. When they were building the Metro in the sixties and seventies, they connected to these tunnels and erected blast doors in the deepest tunnels. They were supposed to protect people if there was a nuclear war. They say there are even hospitals and supplies in the tunnels, but I've never seen them and I've been through most of the tunnels." The breeze whistled through the opening as the train raced toward them. The sound filled the space to a deafening roar and stirred up dust that nearly choked Nicole. She barely heard Jakub shout, "*Go!*" once the train sped past. He grabbed her hand and she grabbed Adam's, and they fled the tunnel, carefully avoiding the rail, and then ran down the path in the center. Jakub's long stride skipped every other tie, but Nicole and Adam paced from one tie to the next like stepping stones.

The draft as the train pulled away from the station sucked at their clothes, pulling them forward.

"Hurry! The next train will be coming soon!" Jakub urged them on. She saw the light ahead beckoning from the station at Jiřího z Poděbrad. But she also could hear the sound of the train coming, could feel the humming in the ties as it approached. Her legs pumped faster, and she tugged at Adam to hurry him along. Lungs burning, she saw the platform now.

Twenty paces away. Ten. The train roared, and its bright light cast her shadow on the wall ahead as Jakub reached the steps. He placed his hands on the platform and vaulted onto the concrete, turning to reach for Adam. Nicole hefted her little brother over her head into Jakub's arms before Adam had time to protest. She pulled herself up the steps and flung herself onto the floor of the platform face first, bending her knees like she was sliding in to home plate, just as the train screeched to a halt, her legs barely clearing the space now occupied by the car.

The platform was virtually empty at this hour, and the few occupants were too weary to cast them more than a curious glance. The three lay on the cool cement, panting for air, until the combination of adrenaline, terror, and intense relief left them laughing hysterically. As the other travelers boarded the subway and the train pulled out, they were finally able to catch their breath.

"So I thought we were going to avoid using the Metro?" Nicole raised an eyebrow at Jakub.

"I sure will from now on," Adam vowed as he broke into another round of laughter.

"We need to find a place where we can hide while you charge your phone and send the files. Then we can return to the church. It's only a block away."

With the station empty, she scanned the platform, but clearly, it was not planned with 21st century cell phone charging in mind. The shiny, beige, tiled walls arched inward near the ceiling and ended with a foot rail where the wall met the floor, a clear expanse uninterrupted by outlets.

"But there are no outlets. How can I charge my phone?"

"There is a café on the corner, near the church. We should be able to find a place there without being seen."

As they approached the café, Nicole understood why they wouldn't be spotted there. Calling it a café was generous. The windows were cluttered with torn and faded posters advertising cigarettes, and the smell of smoke nearly choked her when Jakub opened the door. *Does he really think I'm going inside this dive? I'd rather go back in the tunnels.* She wrinkled her nose and gave him the stink eye.

"Couldn't we see if there is an outlet in the church that would work?"

"You saw the way it was burned. Anything that wasn't damaged by the fire would have been ruined by the water when they put it out."

Nicole waited another moment, trying to think of a more acceptable solution, but none came to mind. Jakub gestured grandly for them to enter and then led them up the narrow stairs to the café. The tiny lamps on each table revealed a room full of characters straight from a Dickens novel. Smoke hung in the air like a fog, obscuring any clear view. They would definitely not be spotted, that was for sure. Jakub led them to a table in the corner. He reached under the table along the wall and found an outlet for the cord. She snapped the other end of the cord into her cell phone until she heard the familiar tone signaling it was connected and charging.

A waitress approached, and she quickly removed her phone from sight and slipped it under the table into her lap. The waitress ignored Nicole and Adam and asked Jakub what they would like. He ordered three Fantas. The young woman returned with the three tepid bottles of orange soda and then left them alone.

Nicole pulled the phone out. *Five percent power.*

Enough to see she had a text message from Sam. It had been weeks since they had talked, but it seemed like years after all she'd been through.

Saw the news. You okay? She laughed but not because it was funny.

No, not really.

She pulled up the internet on her phone and went to the International Mission Force website. She posted a quick update about the situation in Prague and then attached the files from the flash drive. With the phone connected to the power source, the upload went faster than she expected. By the time they had finished their warm sodas, the message had been sent.

"We can go now. I sent the files. Now, it is out of my hands."

Jakub raised his eyebrows, and she knew he was thinking it never had been in her hands. *True enough.*

Jakub left the money for their drinks on the table and the three left the café. The city air seemed fresh and clean compared to the smog of the café.

They slipped into the burnt out church and down the stairs to the store room. Jakub clicked on his flashlight as soon as they were out of sight from the street and led them back to the cave Adam and Nicole had landed in the night before. She was thankful for the light to guide them and the route which did not deposit them in the cold water.

As they emerged into the cavern, Pastor Michal and the others greeted them. He grasped Jakub's forearm and pulled him into a hug, pounding his back with gusto.

"Thank you, thank you, my son! I knew you

would bring these two back to us safely!" He pulled Nicole and Adam into the group hug as well. "What would I have told your parents if you had been captured or hurt? You are too headstrong for your own good." He scolded them, but his smile said they were already forgiven.

It had been only twenty-four hours since they slipped out of the cave. They related their story for the small band of refugees, ending with their narrow escape on the platform of the subway station.

A little girl about five years old began singing a hymn in Czech, and soon, other voices joined hers. Nicole didn't know the Czech words, but recognized the tune and sang in English. Adam joined in as well. The cave echoed with the song. Nicole's gaze wandered from one person to the next as tears streamed down their faces.

Her throat tightened and she bowed her head, unable to get the words out for a moment. The praise continued until Pastor Michal finally raised his arms and prayed.

"Lord, we could worship you for eternity for all your blessings upon us. We know, in these difficult times, you have shown yourself faithful to your people. We ask now that you continue to watch over and protect our loved ones, use this situation to draw others to your Son, and give us rest so we might serve you according to your will tomorrow! Amen."

The people dispersed and sought a place to curl up on the floor. They huddled in groups under the blankets available and used one another as pillows to rest their heads. Nicole knelt by the pool and splashed the cold water on her face, scrubbing the day's grime off with her hands while avoiding the bandage on her forehead. She ran her wet fingers through her hair, slowly working the knots out. *What I wouldn't give for a pony tail holder to pull it out of my face. Or even better, some shampoo.* She pushed aside the complaint and forcibly turned her thoughts back to thankfulness for the success God had given them.

She found Adam curled up, sound asleep, his head resting on Jakub's knees. Jakub dozed, sitting up against the wall of the cave, his chin resting on his chest and one hand resting protectively on Adam's shoulder. She sat down next to her little brother and tried to sleep sitting up, as Jakub was, but found the rocks behind her back too uncomfortable. She slid down to curl around Adam and rested her head on his side, wrapping her arm around him and curling her legs up behind his. As she drifted off to sleep, she imagined a hand stroking her hair and then resting lightly on her shoulder. Visions of God's protection and provision gave way to dreams of desperate prayers.

Josefov, Prague, Bohemia
February 10, 1578 anno domino
Rabbi Ben Loew lit a candle on the rough-hewn table and stared across the space at his two students, the only witnesses to his unholy act. The only ones who knew the truth behind the terror that stalked the streets of Praha by night. His intentions had been so honorable, so noble. He only desired to protect God's people from the tyranny of Emperor Rudolf II. But now, instead of fearing the Emperor's Army,

Jacob's remnant in Praha lived in fear of the Rabbi's minion.

Josef had continued to grow with each passing day, and yet his mind seemed that of a child. Unable to speak, he vented his frustration with physical attacks on anyone who crossed him. And like a recalcitrant child, he no longer heeded the Rabbi's guidance.

"Rabbi, what will we do? The creature is out of control. The people are frightened." The young man's face was pale and drawn. The burden of his secret had aged him beyond his years.

The elderly Rabbi bowed his head and whispered, "We must return him from whence he came."

The two students leaned in to catch his words and then retreated as their meaning soaked in.

Josef Bin Ibrahim spoke for them both once again, "How Father? How can we undo what we have done?"

The Rabbi patted his hand gently. "There is no power we can wield which our Father in heaven cannot overcome. We must fast and pray for wisdom, my sons."

The three knelt together and prayed earnestly for guidance, yet no answer readily appeared. The Rabbi urged them to continue in fasting and to meet each evening to pray for God's intervention. Meanwhile, the golem continued to terrorize the city.

CHAPTER THIRTEEN

Rude Awakening

Nicole's pillow shifted and then vanished, leaving her head to rest on the hard bed. The warm blanket slipped away, and she reached for it in the cool night air. She rolled over and tried to find the blanket, but finally settled for a small pillow she pulled under her cheek as she sighed deeply.

Adam's laughter sounded far away, and she wondered if he were watching a video in the living room. Through foggy dreams, she suspected he had taken her blanket, and she slowly awakened, ready to go and retrieve it.

Her eyes opened to the rough walls of the cave, and her brother stood in front of her, his hand covering a grin as he giggled at her. She raised her head and realized the pillow she had pulled under her head was Jakub's hand.

She jumped as if stung and scooted away, mortified. Adam's quiet chuckle erupted into hysterical laughter as her face flushed crimson. Others in the cave were moving about slowly, beginning their day in prayer or preparing food. They glanced her way at the sound of his laughter, and Nicole rose and clenched her fists to keep from wrapping them around his little neck.

"Shhh! People are still trying to sleep!" she whispered loud enough to wake those still sleeping. Adam covered his mouth to mute his amusement, and she pivoted in time to see Jakub wink at her brother. Adam snickered and danced out of reach before she could dispense some sisterly justice. Glancing nervously over her shoulder to find Jakub grinning at her, she shook her head in irritation and stormed away.

As she approached Pastor Michal, an elderly man hurried towards him.

"Pastor Michal, I was able to slip into the church and get a signal on my cell. I spoke to my brother. The recount is complete. The Communists have lost. The news channel is reporting the military have taken charge and are establishing order and bringing peace to the city."

Within moments, the residents of the cave gathered close and listened as the elderly man relayed the news. The nightmare had ended as quickly and inexplicably as it began. But what would this new twist mean for her parents? She prayed they would be released. She searched the crowd for Adam and found him listening intently as the man continued to relay information from the outside.

She tried to speak to her brother, but he shushed her so he could hear more. When the man finished speaking, Adam translated, "The Communists have taken over the Prague City Hall and won't let the military in. The Army is threatening to attack the building."

Nicole's strength drained out until she sank to her knees on the rough floor. They'd risked their lives to prove their parents were innocent, and now their parents might be killed in the crossfire if the military stormed in to re-establish control! It felt as if she'd plunged again into the pool of water, but this was a flood of despair which threated to drown her.

Deep inside, a tiny knot of resolve grew in her stomach until it consumed her, filling her with strength. She blinked back the tears and pressed her lips together. She had seen God do amazing things in the last two days. Her faith was simply facing another test. And no matter the outcome, God would provide all she needed.

She bowed her head and prayed, "God, you've met our needs through everything. You fed us, clothed us, comforted us, gave us energy to keep going, gave us courage when we were so scared. Please give us what we need to save Mom and Dad. And give us peace that this is in your hands from beginning to end."

She rose slowly with fists braced stiffly at her sides. Her jaw clenched in determination. Adam took a step back, his eyes wide.

"This is not how this ends," she said firmly. She slipped quietly through the crowd until she found Jakub. She pulled him away from the crowd and whispered, "I need your help. You know these tunnels better than anyone. I need to find a way to get to the Prague City Hall."

"Are you crazy? We need to stay here until we are certain it is safe." Jakub tried to reason with her, but she refused to hear his logic. She had to get there before it was too late.

"Jakub, you can either show me the way, or I can try to find it myself and probably get lost, but you can't stop me from going." The steely resolve in her eyes made argument futile. He glanced down at Adam, who stood beside her, eager to follow her on this new quest.

"What about him? Will you put him in danger again? Your parents would want you to protect him, Nicole. If you won't think about your safety, think about his."

His words stung, but she knew he was right. She had freaked out when she lost Adam, and she couldn't put him in jeopardy again. Her chin sank to her chest in defeat, but in her heart she could not give up yet. She'd have to sneak away without him. And, most likely, without Jakub. The thought of wandering through the tunnels without a guide sent a chill to the back of her neck, but she was determined to rescue her parents.

She rested her hand on Adam's shoulder. "He's right. I want to go, but we can't take the chance again. I let you talk me into going out once, but this time, we have to stay here."

He gave her a suspicious sideways glance and strode away in a huff. She watched him storm across the cave and find a spot as far from her as possible to sit and glare at her. She could tell by the shine in his eyes he was fighting back tears.

She pivoted back to Jakub with arms folded and whispered, "I'm going to wait until we eat and he's not watching, but I'm going to go. If you won't go with me, will you at least keep him busy here so he doesn't try to follow me?"

"You are a stubborn girl." His voice hinted at respect as well as irritation with her. His gaze burned with the same intensity that had made her so uncomfortable on the subway a million years ago. The moment stretched at least as long for Nicole as she refused to back down.

Jakub finally glanced down and then met her gaze again, and his expression softened. "What about you? How can I keep him safe here and still protect you as well?"

He no longer simply tried to keep her from leaving. His genuine concern made her cheeks flush, and she was torn between letting him protect her and wanting to save her parents. Her heart was being ripped in two, and her bottom lip trembled. She studied her right foot as it scuffed back and forth on the rough floor of the cave.

When the words came, they were barely audible. "Jakub, I have to go."

"Then you will not be alone." His tone hinted at acceptance of an immovable force. "Wait until I have Adam's attention, then slip into the tunnel out of sight. I will make sure he is busy, and then I will come and find you. Do not try to make it on your own. Promise me you won't do anything foolish." His fingers lifted her chin gently until she had to meet his gaze.

Her heart raced as she answered, "I promise." She

closed her eyes and waited for his lips to meet hers. Her first kiss. Her heart pounded so loudly she feared it might draw attention to them, and her palms felt moist.

But when she opened her eyes, he was halfway across the cave, striding purposefully toward her little brother. The wind had been knocked out of her, and she glanced around to be sure no one had noticed her standing there, eyes closed, lips waiting. Her cheeks burned.

She hurried over to the ladies preparing food and helped as they served the other residents. The food, though monotonous, gave her the energy she needed for the quest. The small bag of food they had brought to the cave fed everyone, yet when they cleaned up the left-overs, the bag still remained half full.

After the meal, she watched Jakub wander toward Adam. He introduced the boy to some of the other children, and one of them produced a deck of cards. Within minutes, they were playing a Czech card game. Adam sat with his back to her. She stole to the entrance of the tunnel past a cluster of people chattering about the good news they'd received and speculating about how long they should wait before returning to their homes. With one last backward glance to be sure no one was watching, she disappeared into the dark labyrinth.

Without the benefit of a flashlight, the darkness in the tunnel shrouded her in gloom. Nicole steadied herself against the brick wall as she squatted and wrapped her arms around her knees. Her imagination conjured monstrous creatures responsible for the scratching, scampering noises that echoed through the passageway. She pushed the nightmarish images away and prayed for wisdom and guidance.

Josefov, Prague, Bohemia
February 17, 1578 anno domino
For the seventh night, the Rabbi and his students met in darkness to pray for God's help against the demon of their own design. Their stomachs spoke almost as fervently as their voices, aching and longing for God to answer their plea for help.

"Father God, hear our cries! Forgive us for our presumptuous sin in thinking we, sinful men, could counterfeit your creative power and bring to life a man. Instead, we have created a dumb brute, incapable of reason, incapable of compassion or understanding. Have mercy on us in our ignorance! Have mercy and help us understand how to right the terrible wrong we have done before it is too late." The Rabbi spoke in hushed whispers broken by pauses as he gasped for air. His body was failing. He recognized the signs of his impending death. With each day, he grew more desperate to correct the mistakes he'd made. With each day, the giant loomed larger, both physically and in his own mind.

His students trembled before him. They had no answers, no wisdom to offer as to how to resolve this problem. Their countenances spoke only of panic and remorse…and to think he had led them down this fools' path. His heart ached over his failure to provide them with godly leadership.

They prayed throughout the night on their knees and finally prostrate, their faces in the dirt, breathing in the dust of the floor, until a faint glow on the horizon warned that morning approached. The Rabbi listened to the hushed still-ness of the community around them. Not a breeze stirred the trees, nor a beast called to its mate in the night.

Then a voice whispered quietly what he must do.

CHAPTER FOURTEEN

Torrent in the Tunnel

How long should I wait? Maybe Jakub couldn't get away from Adam. What if he doesn't come? She squeezed her knees tighter to still her trembling hands. Silent prayers calmed her nerves while she waited. It seemed like hours before she finally heard footsteps of the two-legged variety. She stood up, and her breath escaped with a whoosh when she caught sight of Jakub's face in the yellow glow of a small flashlight.

"Praise the Lord. I was beginning to think you weren't coming."

"Your brother is more observant than I thought. I had to ask a friend to watch him."

"You're right about that. He has eyes in the back of his head." Nicole laughed.

"Perhaps waiting in the dark has changed your mind? Brought sense to you?" His voice sounded hopeful.

"You mean, 'brought me to my senses?' No, it hasn't!"

He shook his head. "Then we should go quickly." And without another word, he set off down the tunnel, the light from his flashlight bouncing off the walls ahead of them. Rain and sewer runoff collected into puddles in the tunnels, and each step splattered dirty water up to her knees.

She found herself scurrying once again to keep up with his pace. Each time they approached a side tunnel, he paused only a moment, as if consulting a mental map of the tunnels, and then strode purposefully in a new direction. *How is he able to keep the myriad turns and intersections straight when each one looks identical?* She had enough trouble finding her way around the city above where landmarks gave each street its own unique charm.

They splashed through the tunnels for miles before he finally stopped beneath a storm drain. The rain had intensified, and water poured through the drain into the tunnels. The once small trickle of water rose to four inches deep and moved quickly, tugging each step backward.

"We have to get out of the tunnel now."

Jakub's tone sent a chill up Nicole's spine. The storm drain presented their only means of escape, and it loomed twenty-five feet over their heads. They examined the sides of the tunnel for any means to climb up to the grate. But even as she searched, doubt about whether they could lift the heavy grate, even if they reached it, gnawed at her confidence.

The waterfall cascaded down the vertical wall of the storm drain, broken at regular intervals by bricks jutting out about three inches—a built-in ladder leading up to the grate. Although the steps provided meager support, they would have been sufficient if not for the water pouring down over them.

Their gazes met, and she read the desperation in Jakub's dark eyes. "How can we climb it with all that water?" she shouted over the sound of rushing water. At their feet, it now rose to their ankles. She was amazed at the pressure the flowing water exerted and the effort it took to remain standing. She knew, within moments, the water would sweep them both away, through the tunnels and eventually into the Vltava River.

"It is our only chance," Jakub said grimly. "You go first."

"Jakub, I can't. There is no way I will be able to move the grate on the storm drain. You have to go first!"

He didn't hesitate or argue but quickly approached the wall and began climbing. As soon as his feet were above her head, Nicole grabbed a brick below him and began climbing. His body diverted most of the water, allowing her an easier climb. She imagined it must take all of his strength to hold on to the bricks with the water flowing over them. A glance up at Jakub brought a surge of admiration as he continued upward despite the water splashing in his face and rushing over his hands.

He reached the grate and tucked his head, pressing up on the grate with his shoulder and upper back. She watched the muscles in his hands and neck tighten as he strained to cling to the wall while trying to move the heavy metal grid. A scraping noise revealed his progress as the grate moved an inch, then another inch. As the grill lifted free of its setting, he shifted his weight and heaved the grate six inches to the side. Nicole peeked down to see water nearly filling the tunnel where they had stood a moment before. As it rushed past, she knew if she lost her grip on the brick above her head, she would be carried away by the current.

She watched Jakub as he struggled to move the grate a second time.

"You can do it! Push, Jakub, push!" Nicole urged him on as the water below rose and the water from above splattered in her face. The water sprayed her already-soaked legs as it filled the tunnel below completely, splashing as it hit the vertical wall of the storm drain. It rose quickly toward her feet in a swirling brown mass.

Jakub grunted as he pressed on the grate again. One more effort would give them the space they needed to escape the raging torrent below. Nicole prayed aloud, "Lord, give him the strength…give him the strength…give him the strength!" She gasped as the grate lifted free and Jakub flung it to the side. He quickly climbed out and reached back to help her.

As soon as his body cleared the opening, she was no longer protected from the deluge, and the water pounded at her hands and sprayed her in the face. Her fingers slipped to the edge of the brick and the stream of water hid the next handhold. She sputtered and tried to cry out as the water poured over her, but the flood filled her mouth, silencing her cries. She could see Jakub's hand reaching down, but it was far beyond her reach.

Gasping for breath, she reached blindly for the next brick, gripping it with the tips of her fingers. As she tried to lift her right foot to the next step, the water pushed her other foot off the ledge, and she clung to the wall by the fingertips of one hand. A scream tore from her throat as her free hand and legs flailed about. Far away, she heard the sound of her name echoing through the tunnel. Her fingers ached as she tried to grip the wall, but the water pushed at them, trying to dislodge her grasp. As her grip slipped, she took a deep breath, certain that a split second later, she would be tumbling down into the maelstrom.

Instead, the water below rushed upward, soaking her as it pushed toward the only available space. She rocketed up through the tunnel as if she'd been shot from a canon, and landed with a thud in a heap on the cobblestone square of Old Town as the water over-flowed the drain. It was still dark, and the rain beat down on them as they both lay panting for air.

Finally, Nicole found the strength to lift herself onto her hands and knees and look down at Jakub. His hands covered his face, and his shoulders shook as he cried out to God, "Oh bože, ne ! Ne !" *Oh God. No! No!*

She pulled his hands away and read tortured grief in his face.

He stared at her a moment before a glimmer of recognition lit his eyes. His expression melted from pain to joy. "I could not reach you. I tried so hard…but you were too far down. When I saw you lose your grip, I could not watch."

He pulled her to him and crushed her against his chest. Their tears mixed with the rain pouring down. She nestled her head against his chest and wanted to stay there forever, but reality called. They rose slowly, and Nicole realized they were essentially back where they had started twenty-four hours ago, in Old Town, across the square from St. Nicholas Church.

"How are we going to find the City Hall now?" she asked. "And then how will we find our way back to the others? We definitely can't use the tunnels again." She shivered at the thought.

Jakub was silent, his face drained of color. It took Nicole only a moment to realize his concern. The water had filled up the tunnels. Adam and their friends were hiding in a cave connected to the same system of tunnels. Without warning, the inhabitants of the cave would have no time to escape.

"Jakub, what about Adam and Pastor Michal and the others? They'll all drown if we don't get to them. We've got to warn them!" Panic rose as quickly as the water had.

"There is no way to reach them." His voice was barely a whisper. "There is no time. The water is already there, even now." His head sank to his chest. Her knees weakened and would have collapsed if he had not held her up. He wrapped his arm around her waist and half-carried her out of the middle of the square toward a side street as she sobbed hysterically.

"There are soldiers patrolling the streets. We can't be certain they are on our side. We still must be careful. Think about your parents, not the others, right now," he whispered in her ear.

She tried to control her grief, but her shoulders lurched intermittently as she sucked in gulps of air.

A soldier in camouflage raingear approached, a machine gun slung carelessly over his shoulder, and asked something her stunned brain couldn't translate. Jakub replied, his words slurred and followed by a loud guffaw. The soldier frowned but motioned them on. She eyeballed Jakub as if he'd taken leave of his senses, but allowed him to continue to maneuver her until the soldier was out of sight.

"What was that all about?"

"The soldier asked if you were all right and I told him you had too much to drink and I was taking you home."

They ducked into a narrow alley shielded from the blowing rain by the buildings on either side while she struggled to control the overwhelming flood of fear.

"What do we do now?" Her voice sounded hollow in her own ears. It didn't matter anymore. She had left Adam, and now he was drowned, along with Pastor Michal and the others.

"Nicole," said Jakub, "if it weren't for you, we would be drowned as well. Your parents will be glad you escaped, and they will know you were trying to protect Adam and to help them."

She nodded but didn't trust herself to speak. Bracing herself against the gray stone wall, she covered her face with her hands. It was too much. She couldn't take another step, didn't dare to hope she could free her parents. *God, how could this have happened?* Her shoulders shook as a wave of emotion swept over her, more powerful than the one she had faced in the tunnel below. Jakub put his arms around her, and she leaned in to him and let the tears flow. He cradled her head against his chest until her cries dwindled down to sniffles.

She would keep going, focus on helping her parents and not on what might have happened to Adam and the others. She drew a long breath and gazed up at Jakub with all the resolve she could muster.

"How far are we from Prague City Hall?"

"Four blocks, perhaps. We must get to the other side of the square, past St. Nicholas and down Platnerska to Marianski Namesti, the Czech National Library. The City Hall is across the street from the library. Do you have a plan once we get there?" Jakub ran his hand through his wet hair and water splattered to the ground.

"Well, sort of." She hesitated. "My plan was for us to get to Prague City Hall. Beyond that, I'm praying for God to do a miracle."

"He has certainly done many miracles for us today."

Nicole silenced the voice of doubt which said they needed at least two more.

They stayed close to the buildings, sheltered by the eaves from the dwindling rain, and moved from one entrance alcove to the next to avoid the soldiers patrolling the area. Their progress was slow as they circled around the Old Town square without being detected.

The early morning light transformed the sky from black to charcoal gray. In the shadows, she saw a tiny wrinkled man under an umbrella on the street corner with a small stack of newspapers. He held one paper aloft and called to them in Czech. She shook her head and avoided eye contact as they approached the corner, but she suddenly recognized the couple on the front page. *My parents!* Their faces were pale and frightened and their arms were pinned behind them as they were being led out of a jail cell. Her mother's head was wrapped in a bandage. She tugged at Jakub's arm and whispered to him.

"It's my parents."

Jakub fished in his pocket to retrieve a few coins, pressed them into the hand of the old man, and took the paper the man offered. He quickly scanned the article as he and Nicole turned the corner and paused for a moment.

"It says, 'Americký bez.' It means 'Americans Innocent.' The newspaper received the computer information we sent. They say it is being reported throughout the world that they are innocent. The United Nations says it will issue sanctions if they are not freed immediately." She stared at him incredulously.

"We did it. We really did it." Her voice sounded hollow and flat. She couldn't celebrate, not until her parents were safe. And not when the thought of her brother, Pastor Michal, and the others chilled her heart.

The closer they drew to the City Hall, the greater the military presence grew. Jakub led her from the shadows of one doorway to the next until at last, they peered from the entrance of the National Library to the City Hall across the street. Jeeps surrounded the building, and a tank sat in the parking lot, its turret aimed at the arched entrance. Loudspeakers blasted warnings at those inside.

Nicole scanned the elaborate façade which seemed more like a museum than a municipal government building. Stone figures adorned the roof with a copper dome, aged to a green patina, rising above them. Granite stairs led up to a huge, dark, wooden double door under the stone arch. Above the entrance, two flags flew on a balcony and the corners of the building were arched inward to form decorative alcoves. In the corner alcove nearest them stood a bronze statue of a faceless giant, the Prague golem. Protector of the persecuted. Avenger of the oppressed.

Soldiers squatted behind their vehicles with weapons drawn, waiting for the signal from their commander to proceed.

Nicole and Jakub ducked back into the alley to formulate a plan.

"They have a tank." Jakub whispered urgently. "Now would be a good time for a miracle."

She knelt on the wet cobblestones and reached for Jakub's hand. He stooped beside her as she prayed, "Lord, you have led us all this way. You have clothed us. You have fed us. Lord, you have provided everything at just the moment we needed it. Help us to know what we should do. We can't do this on our own. We need you to show yourself mighty right now."

Though her eyes were squeezed tight, light penetrated her lids as if the sun had suddenly broken through the clouds. She opened her eyes and squinted against the brilliance of an army of angels filling the street, each one glowing with clean, white light and armed with swords of radiant gold. She squeezed Jakub's hand. "Look up!"

His eyes grew round with awe as the army of God surrounded them. Nicole scanned from the angelic army to Jakub's stunned gaze and smiled. An image from the pages of her history book sprang to mind: A single protester standing in defiance before a long line of tanks in Tiananmen Square. She knew immediately what she must do.

"I have to go alone," she told Jakub. She pointed toward the angelic warriors. "They will go with me, but you must stay here." She pressed her phone into his hand. "Stay here and videotape what happens. And pray that I have understood God correctly!" She didn't give him time to protest, or herself time to second-guess, but darted out into the street. A rush of wind swept her hair from her face as the army of God surrounded her. She strode across the street, arms at her sides, fists tight, until she reached the steps of the old building directly in front of the tank.

The soldiers watched her, bruised and grimy and soaked to the skin, as she planted her feet resolutely before their forces. She knew their unbelieving eyes saw only a teenage girl, and yet she stood with such determination, they seemed paralyzed. She remained silent, the rain misting over her. Finally, a man in uniform approached, his chest covered in medals and his olive hat lined with four gold stars. He spoke in Czech, but she understood every word. He ordered her to move out of their way.

"These men have caused much trouble, but they will not be able to cause any more trouble. Ever again."

The cold look in his eyes told her there would be no mercy for those who had initiated this chaos. For a moment, she considered simply pleading for her parents' lives and then letting them flatten the building and everyone else inside. The police deserved to pay for all the pain they had caused over the last three days. Her mind recalled each story she had heard of the brutality and cruelty caused by those same public servants who currently held her parents' lives in their hands. But the command echoed in her mind, "Love your enemies."

"No," she said in perfect Czech. "You will not kill these men."

He stepped back, evidently appalled at her nerve in defying him.

"You will let them surrender and stand trial. If you don't, you're no different than they are."

His gaze locked hers and she gritted her teeth, determined not to back down. Her eyes flicked down for an instant and the name on his uniform came into sharp focus. Ruzicka.

Her mind raced back to her first weeks in Prague, to her friendship with Eliska...and to her abandonment of the lonely girl. And then to the last week and Eliska's willingness to forgive her and renew their friendship. With sudden clarity, she saw how she had treated the other girl, her cruelty and selfishness, like a knife slicing her own heart. Silently, she cried out to God for forgiveness while outwardly, she remained steadfast. *Should I apologize to him for treating his daughter so cruelly? Does he already know who I am or would confessing to him only make the situation worse?*

She wrestled with her conscience for only a second.

"General Ruzicka, I'm Nicole Wise. Your daughter, Eliska, is a friend of mine. I mean, she welcomed me as her friend, and then I treated her terribly. But she still accepted me, even when everyone else turned against me. She forgave me when she didn't have to. She gave me a chance to change, to make it right. Can't you give them that chance?"

As the sun peeked through the gloom over the roof of the library, it shone like a spotlight on her face. Nicole saw the angel army encircle her and for a moment, she wondered if the general saw them as well. He took another step back, blinking against the brightness. Whether it was the brilliance of the sun or the host of heaven blinded him, she couldn't tell, but he shouted to his men.

"Put down your weapons! Do not fire!"

He faced her, standing three steps below her with his hands shielding his eyes from the glare. "We will do it!"

"Tell them to come out now," she said calmly.

He spoke into his cell phone, and she heard the command broadcast over the loudspeaker. She spun to see the doors of the station open and officers stream out, their hands raised in submission. As they descended the steps, squinting against the blinding light, the soldiers approached and handcuffed them.

Nicole sprinted past them through the giant wooden doors. A million questions crowded her mind but only one mattered. *Am I too late?*

CHAPTER FIFTEEN

Love Wins

Nicole raced into the building. The sudden shift from brilliant light to shadows blinded her, and she smashed into the firm chest of a burly police officer. He shoved her to the side and continued his flight. Momentum carried her, stumbling, across the room where she hit the wall with a grunt as the air was knocked from her. She caught her breath and waited until the fleeing officers and staff left the building, searching their ranks for her parents.

She saw neither her parents nor Mara's father. *What if they aren't here? What if I came all this way to the wrong station or they have been moved? What if I'm simply too late?* She clenched her jaw, determined not to let her fears overtake her as she threw open the first office and peered inside. Cluttered desks huddled together in little clumps under the amber light of wall sconces with no sign of the room's occupants.

She tore through the other offices, slamming doors open and searching desperately for her mother and father. Satisfied they were not on that floor, she took the elevator to the second level.

The elevator doors opened on a formal reception area, no doubt the executive suite. Vacant like the rest. *Where are the holding cells?* She started to push the button to go to the next floor but froze as voices resounded from behind the office door.

"Tata, ne!" *Daddy, No!* The girl's desperate cry chilled her blood. It was Mara.

Nicole dashed halfway across the reception area before her father's calm, steady voice grabbed her heart. "Please, let my wife go. Let her leave with your daughter, and you and I can resolve this. I don't want anyone to get hurt."

They're here. Her parents were both in the next room with Mara and her father. The weight of her own decisions paralyzed her. If she made the wrong move, waited too long or rushed in too soon, it could mean their lives. Her heart searched for guidance while she scanned the room for a weapon. Her courage seemed to have stayed behind at the front door with the heavenly army.

The sleek lines of the contemporary furniture in the reception area stood in defiance of the century-old architecture and offered little in the way of defense. A blond-maple receptionist desk faced three matching chairs. She tried to snatch one up over her head to use as a weapon, but let out a grunt when the heavy chair wouldn't budge.

The door behind her creaked as it swung open, and she pivoted to see Mara's father glaring with murderous intent as he leveled a gun at her. He was beside her before she could react, his strong hand a vice on her bicep as he dragged her into the room.

"What have we here?" He sneered as he spoke with a heavy accent. "What a nice time for a family reunion, eh?" He pushed her toward her parents.

Her father's arms wrapped around her like a constrictor, cutting off her oxygen.

"Dad, not so tight!" she squeaked.

Her mother joined the hug as tears flowed down their faces. She brushed a kiss to the bruise on Nicole's forehead. "Are you all right?" Nicole laughed at the absurdity of the question in their current circumstance.

"Enough!" Novak shouted.

Her father pulled Nicole and her mother behind him gently and faced off against the man. "Yes, Senator. It is enough. You must give yourself up before the army loses patience. They have us surrounded and could storm the building at any moment. You may not care about my family, but think of your family…"

"My family? How dare you speak of my family? You know nothing."

"Tata, please," Mara begged. "What will I do without you?"

Nicole ached for the pain etched on her friend's face.

"I've already lost your mother. I cannot bear to lose you. They have stolen your heart away from me." His hardened face crumbled like an earthen vessel under intense pressure.

"Tata, ne. They have stolen nothing. I have given my heart freely to Jesus, but it is not lost to you, Tata." She eased closer to him and laid her hand on his arm.

His jaw worked back and forth as he seemed to war within himself. "You don't understand. Western religion, their preoccupation with freedom, it leads to nothing but destruction. You are just like your mother. She wanted this Western freedom and it cost her life!"

Mara jerked her hand back as if scalded and her mouth gaped. "What do you mean? You told me she became sick. You told me she died in childbirth because she was ill."

"It was a sickness! A disease. This longing for freedom. First, she wanted to attend classes at the University. And I allowed it, because I loved her. Then there were the meetings with other students. American students. She would come home speaking of freedom. Challenging everything we believed. I did not know what they were planning. I did not know." His voice broke and his hand drifted downward as if the weight of the gun were too much for him.

"What, Tata? What were they planning?" Mara faced him and clung to his arms as she begged him to unearth his secret.

"Sametova Revoluce." Barely a whisper, yet the words unleashed a flood of anguish held back for over a decade. His face twisted in grief and hatred.

"But no one died in the Velvet Revolution. We learned about it in school. It was peaceful," Mara stammered in confusion.

"Ne. Your mother did not die that day. But she suffered a blow to her head. Damage to her brain. The doctor delivered you, my daughter, but could not save her." His left hand cupped her face. Guilt clouded his expression, and he looked away. "I was so ashamed of her, I told the doctor she had been assaulted on her way home. I did not want anyone to know what she had done."

A shadow shifted in the doorway behind Mara and her father, and Nicole squeezed her father's hand to draw his attention. A black muzzle edged through the doorway and lined up with the Senator as he and his daughter embraced. As they separated, Novak lifted the gun again, this time reaching toward the desk in front of him, his fingers limp, the gun hanging uselessly upside down.

A blast erupted from muzzle in the doorway and the Senator crumpled as he dropped the gun onto the desk. Half a dozen soldiers poured into the space, their weapons trained on Nicole and her parents. The three of them stood with arms raised as Mara sank to the floor crying and pulled her father's head into her lap. He coughed and clutched at his gut where thick red blood spread across his shirt.

General Ruzicka strode into the room, shouting for his men to lower their weapons. At the General's instruction, the soldiers dragged Mara away and pressed their bare hands against the Senator's wound to staunch the flow of blood while his daughter stood watching.

Nicole pulled away from her parents and ran to her friend. Three days of separation seemed like a lifetime. She wrapped her arms around her friend and held her while she sobbed. Her parents joined them, murmuring prayers for the Senator's life and thanksgiving for their own safety.

A soldier interrupted to whisper to her father. "We will take him to the hospital."

"Will he survive?"

Nicole strained to hear the man answer.

"Mozna." Perhaps.

Her father told the man they would bring Mara to the hospital as soon as possible. The moment had come to tell them about Adam. Her heart plummeted as she tried to find the words.

"Daddy, we have to go to the church first. Adam was there, in the cave beneath the church, and we think it flooded."

"What cave?"

"Why was Adam at the church?

Her parents both spoke at once, hammering her with questions until she raised her hands and shushed them.

"We found Pastor Michal and some of the church members hiding in a cave underneath the church. Jakub and I escaped through a tunnel to come and find you and then the tunnel filled with water." She took a deep breath and continued. "We need to get to the church as quickly as possible."

As the paramedics lifted the Senator onto a gurney, Nicole grabbed Mara's hand and slipped past them into the elevator. Her parents followed close behind. They stepped out of the elevator just as Jakub burst through the open doorway.

"Nicola!" He ran to her and grabbed her in a bear hug, lifting her off her feet. "I heard the gunshot…" His voice trailed off.

She held on tight until she noticed her parents' raised eyebrows. She pulled away and awkwardly introduced Jakub to her parents.

"Mom, Dad, this is Jakub. He helped us prove you

were innocent." She brought Jakub up to speed. "A soldier shot Mara's father. He reached to put his gun down, but they were behind him and thought he was going to shoot us. They're taking him to the hospital, and Mara needs to go with him, but Jakub, we have to get to the church. We have to find out if Adam and the others got out somehow."

General Ruzicka emerged from the elevator followed by two paramedics pushing a gurney with the Senator. Nicole seized his arm as he passed them.

"General, please. My friend needs to be with her father, but we have to get to the church on Jiriho z Podebrad. Can you help us?"

The General barked orders to two soldiers nearby, then gestured for Mara to go with one and Nicole and her family to follow the other.

As they neared the doorway, the light outside filled the portal with a blinding glow. But the moment they stepped through, the light faded to normal sunshine peeking through the clouds of a summer morning. She blinked as her vision adjusted to the change. She surveyed the square, but no evidence remained of the angelic army, only soldiers in drab gray rubbing their eyes as the clouds parted.

The soldier led them to a jeep parked around the corner from City Hall, and the foursome climbed in. News that the standoff had ended must be trickling out slowly. The driver seemed to understand the urgency as he careened through the empty streets. With no traffic to battle, they reached the church in minutes. The jeep slowed in front of the burned-out church and they leapt out and scurried through the damaged sanctuary. Nicole's heart raced, and she clung to Jakub's hand as he led them down the narrow staircase. She inhaled deeply despite the acrid air, trying to calm her nerves, and watched as he pushed against the door to the secret room.

CHAPTER SIXTEEN

Miraculous Delivery

The door wouldn't budge. Nicole's father came alongside Jakub and the two pushed at the raised panels, trying to get the door to slide into its pocket. Finally, they heard a tiny click and the door slid back an inch. Then another inch. An audible gasp came from inside the room and Nicole's heart jumped like she'd been shocked.

"It's them. They're alive!" She joined Jakub and her father, pushing on the jammed door until it opened wide enough for her to squeeze through. She pushed on the table wedged against the door and, once free, the door slid into its place in the wall. Her heart raced as she scanned the faces packed into the small room. An uproar greeted her as recognition and relief dawned on the refugees.

"It's over. It's safe for you to return home now!" She shouted to be heard over the din. Nicole's parents and Jakub followed her through the opening and stepped to the side as the first people rushed up the stairs.

"Nicola, you are alive! God is so good!" Pastor

Michal waved from behind the mob, which moved as one body toward the open door.

She pressed through the group to the old pastor and wrapped her arms around his neck. Her knees buckled and she would have fallen if not for the arms holding her as the throng parted to reveal her little brother, his own eyes filled with tears. She let go of the pastor and hurried to him, barely daring to believe her sight. She grabbed his skinny arms and pulled him close as her parents encompassed the two of them in their arms.

By the time Nicole opened her eyes, only the six of them remained in the room—her family, Pastor Michal, and Jakub.

"How...I mean, how could you possibly..." She couldn't bear to actually put her fears into words.

"I followed you," Adam began. "But after a while, I couldn't see the light up ahead anymore. The water started to get deeper and I got scared. I screamed your name, but when you didn't come back for me, I started back to the cave. I had a little flashlight Pavel gave me. Plus, I was able to run because I don't have to bend over in the tunnel." For the first time, he seemed pleased about his size. "I told Pastor Michal about the water, and by that time, it was getting deep in the cave, too. The pool had already spilled over the edge. So he led us all here to higher ground!"

"If he had been moments later, we might not have had time to get everyone to safety. But Adam is the hero. He saved us all! Praise God." The white-haired man shook his head slowly. "And I had just noticed them missing and wondered where they had wandered off to this time!"

"'This time?'" Her father frowned at her.

Nicole, Jakub, and Adam exchanged a glance and then burst out laughing. "We'll talk about it later." She spoke for them all as her parents looked at each other in confusion. *It's over. The nightmare is finally over.*

Josefov, Prague, Bohemia
February 18, 1578 anno domino
Rabbi Ben Loew and his two companions followed the golem at a safe distance. Josef lumbered through the darkened streets. Anyone he encountered ran in terror at the mere sight of him. Pity the man emboldened by ale who chose to stand his ground. At least two had already met their maker this night alone. The rabbi swiped at the traces of tears with the sleeve of his robe, overcome by remorse for his reckless creation.

The sound of hoof beats on the cobblestones clattered into his brain as he saw his minion stumble into the street just as the Emperor's guards rode in. The horses danced nervously as the giant towered over their heads. The three men lurked in the shadows, watching.

Von Rumpf, recovered from his beating, led the guard and ordered one of the lower ranking members to subdue the beast with a rope. The poor boy couldn't have been more than sixteen and might as well have been asked to secure the moon. His face glowed pale in the night as he timidly approached the golem, his mount uncooperative. The golem swung one arm wide, knocking the boy and the horse to the street in one blow. The other guardsmen gasped and nudged their horses back a length. The fallen horse screamed in pain until *Von Rumpf* ended its suffering. The boy lay still on the cobblestones.

Von Rumpf would not be deterred. He tossed an end of rope to the man next to him, who grabbed it without hesitation as the chamberlain spurred his mount into a tight circle just outside the golem's reach. Once, twice, three times around, and then *Von Rumpf* pulled the rope tight, securing the hulk's arms to his sides. He quickly circled several more times until the entire length of rope had the golem immobilized from the waist up. *Von Rumpf* jumped lightly to his feet and approached the golem to secure the ropes, but when he came within reach, *Josef* raised his massive arms and the ropes shredded like ancient parchment.

Rabbi *Judah Ben Loew* crouched in a corner of the cellar, his cloak gathered around his frail body as he shivered in the dark. The golem should return shortly from his evening raid. *Ben Loew* prayed fervently the damage the hulk caused would be minimal and no more lives would be lost. That had been his prayer often over the past week as he sought guidance from *Yahweh* each night on how to end his creation's reign of terror.

The answer had finally come, and he tried not to analyze what the cost of his folly might be. Which was more a threat to his people, the golem or the Emperor? He had sent his students home, urging them to pray for him as he sought to carry out his plan.

A sound from the steps drew his attention to where the golem lumbered down to the cellar. He waited in the shadows until the beast had settled himself on the pallet on the floor. When *Josef* lay still, *Ben Loew* crept up beside him. His fingers pried the clay lips open and removed the scroll from *the golem's mouth. A breath escaped the monster's mouth like the hissing of a pot steaming over an open fire, and then the clay man was no more.*

Mara's text had been cryptic, but urgent. Nicole clenched and released her hands as she stood outside the guarded hospital room door. Beyond this door lay the monster who had threatened to destroy her family. Her parents insisted on coming with her and stood nearby and, for once, she did not mind their watchful eyes. Independence wasn't all it was cracked up to be.

The door swung inward and her friend's wan smile welcomed her in. The uniformed man at the door tipped his head to give approval.

She didn't know what to expect. *Mara seems glad to see me, but why here? Why now?*

Mara grabbed her by the hand and pulled her past the curtain to where the Senator lay in the bed. At first, Nicole thought he was dead. His face was ashen and his chest barely moved. Her breath caught in her throat when he turned his head, and his eyelids parted ever so slightly. His hand, trailing a tube leading to the IV, flicked in her direction which she took as a gesture beckoning her closer. She stepped near the bed as his raspy voice croaked unintelligible words.

She cast a glance at Mara and raised her shoulders, shaking her head. Her friend came alongside her and placed her hand on Nicole's arm. "He wants to tell you something. Go ahead, Tata."

"Děkuji…Zachránil jsi mi život… Mám stát křesťanem." His dry lips barely moved as the words came out one at a time.

She eyed her friend uncertainly. She heard what he said, but wondered if she had understood him correctly.

Mara smiled, "He says, 'thank you, you saved my life. I have become a Christian.'"

Nicole stared at her friend. She tried to absorb the words but couldn't quite trust her ears. Mara's grin widened.

"It's true. When he came out of surgery, I kept talking to him. I didn't know what to say, so I told him what I had learned from you, and how I felt such peace now. I didn't even think he could hear me, but then he opened his eyes and there were tears in them. He said, 'Chci ten klid, než zemřu'—'I want that peace before I die.'" Mara's voice broke with emotion.

"And he actually put his faith in Christ?" Nicole hated the doubt she heard in her own voice, but it seemed impossible God could change such a bitter heart in so short a time.

"Yes." She sobbed as she reached out to grip her father's hand.

"This is so amazing. What has the doctor said? Is he going to be all right?"

Mara didn't meet her gaze. Nicole strained to hear her answer.

"They don't know."

She hugged her friend and promised to pray for the Senator. "My parents will be praying for him, too. I know they will be so thrilled to hear the news." She squeezed Mara's hand as she turned to go. "Let us know if you need anything." Her friend nodded but didn't say a word.

Nicole's mind reeled as she stepped into the hallway. God's plan included so much more than she had imagined. The thought hit her again and again, like waves crashing on the sand. It wasn't about her parents. It wasn't about an election, or a coup, or a band of survivors. Or maybe it was about all of those things, but it was also about this one man. One man who didn't know Christ and who Christ loved enough to die for. Everything she had been through had worked together to achieve the salvation of this one man.

Nicole drummed anxiously on the back of the seat as the metro pulled into the station near her school. She had spent the weekend resting and enjoying the time with her family. Less than a week had passed since Mara had prayed to receive Christ, yet Nicole felt like she was the one reborn. As she stepped from the train, her last experience on this platform flashed through her mind. Her stomach tightened at the thought of what might await her at the school.

She recalled God's faithfulness in every detail over the past week, and courage welled up inside to face whatever the future might bring. She lifted her chin just a bit and stepped onto the escalator.

As she emerged from the darkness and into the light, the faces of her classmates greeted her. They were waiting for her in a crowd at the top of the escalator. She glanced behind her but people filled the steps. There was nowhere for her to turn and no place to hide. She scanned the faces of her one-time friends but could not read their intentions.

Ondria stood at the front of the crowd with her

arms folded across her chest.

"Well, look who we have here," she said. But instead of approaching, she stepped to the side. Behind her, hidden by the other students, was Mara.

She squealed and ran to her. "How is your father?"

Her red-rimmed eyes filled with tears and her lips pressed tightly together as she shook her head.

"No, oh no!" Nicole wrapped her arms around her friend. "I am so sorry."

Mara sniffed back the tears and worked up a tenuous smile. "He is at peace because of you. Before he died, he told me everything about my mother. About Slane. He confessed he had Slane kidnapped and sold on the black market."

Ondria put her hand on Nicole's shoulder. "I'm sorry. Mara told us everything—how you helped her and how you tried to save her father." She looked down.

Nicole's gut still ached. *Can I truly forgive someone who attacked me only a week ago?* Novak's face came to mind, and with it, the recollection of the bitterness he had held all those years…and how it ultimately hurt the ones he loved and cost him his life.

"Thanks, Ondria. Everything is going to be all right." She smiled at the girl and then pulled her into a hug as well.

"We saw you on television. You were standing in the rain in front of a tank!" Jakub's videotape had gone viral, and it seemed the whole world had seen it. Ondria and the other students crowded around her, asking questions and patting her on the back as if she had won a race. From the victim of a vicious attack to their hero in a span of a week. She shook her head as they swept her along in an impromptu victory parade to the school. Throughout the day, her friends greeted her and strangers hailed her as a celebrity. She was now 'Nádrže–holka', the 'tank-girl'.

Nicole stood at ease on the tram as it lurched through the city streets toward her home. The day looked much like the one a week before except for the changes that had occurred in her heart. Her priorities had changed, her faith had been stretched and beaten down and stretched again until she hardly recognized herself.

She bounded down the steps of the tram onto the street and proceeded up the hill toward the apartment...her home. A familiar face stepped out of the corner shop and blocked her path. Jakub grinned and fell into step beside her.

The computer whirred quietly as Nicole tapped at the keys a few hours later. With a smile, she leaned back in the chair and reviewed the details of her story on the screen, still amazed at all God had done. Her grin widened as her friends in the International Mission Force around the globe posted comments and words of encouragement. Life was good. God was good. All the time.

About the Author

Felicia Bridges began writing as an Army BRAT learning to enjoy life overseas. Her nomadic childhood created a passion for missions and travel that energizes her writing. She is a contributing author for *Then Along Came an Angel: Messengers of Deliverance* and *God's Provision in Tough Times,* a finalist for the 2014 Selah Awards. Serving in ministry for over twenty years alongside her husband,  and the mother of four children, Felicia's vision is to inspire the next generation to carry the gospel to all nations. Her blog focuses on living on mission wherever life's adventure leads and can be found at: www.AdventuresThatInspireAction.wordpress.com.

Felicia graduated with highest honors from North Carolina State University with a B.A. in Psychology and a concentration in Human Resources Development. More than a decade of experience as an HR Manager has sharpened her understanding of people, while providing some very interesting stories. As a Dale Carnegie graduate, she is equally comfortable speaking to the stranger in the checkout line or an auditorium full of people.

Acknowledgments

Thank you first and most of all to the Lord, for putting this idea in my heart and for never letting me set it aside. Thank you for your promise that, "He who began a good work in me, will complete it." This book is proof of the truth found in that promise.

God worked through so many people over the past eleven years to nudge me along this path. At times he used a carrot, and other times a stick, and occasionally he let me rest along the way. But he never let me forget that this was his calling on my life, to write stories that would bring the nations home and inspire future missionaries.

Thank you to Daphne Woodall, my encourager, my conference roomie, my fellow writer, and my best friend. You are the one God used to move my writing from a dream/hobby to a goal, a plan and a reality.

Thank you to Christy and Victoria McQuade —my first readers! Without your enthusiasm for this story, I would surely have given up. You will never know how much it meant to me to hear you say, "I laughed, I cried, I loved it!" Truly an author's favorite response to their work.

Thank you to Cec Murphy—without the scholarship you provided to Blue Ridge Mountain Christian Writers Conference, I would never have learned how much I had yet to learn!

Thank you to my husband and my wonderful kids for your patience with all my hours camped out on the sofa, glued to the laptop, and all the times you had to ask a question twice because it took me a few moments to come home from Prague.

Thank you to my prayer-warrior sisters in The Light Brigade! For praying, for holding me accountable with the simple question, "What have you written this week?" For encouraging me, for providing wisdom and counsel on this crazy journey. I love each of you and can't imagine making this trek without you!

Thank you to my parents, Ltc. (Ret.) Harold and Kathy Bowen, for the gift of being an Army BRAT. By God's design, those years filled with transitions, new cultures, new people, and new experiences forged the foundation for this series—a love of people, an understanding of the challenges of acculturation, a heart for travel and adventure, and a trust in God regardless of circumstances.

Trademark Acknowledgments

The author gratefully acknowledges use of the following trademarks:

Cinnabon - CINNABON LLC LIMITED LIABILITY COMPANY GEORGIA 5620 GLENRIDGE DRIVE ATLANTA GEORGIA 30342

Walt Disney World - Disney Enterprises, Inc. CORPORATION DELAWARE 500 South Buena Vista Street Burbank CALIFORNIA 91521

CNN - CABLE NEWS NETWORK, INC. CORPORATION DELAWARE ONE CNN CENTER, 10N C/O TURNER BROADCASTING SYSTEM, INC. ATLANTA GEORGIA 30303

Food Lion - DZA Brands, LLC LIMITED LIABILITY COMPANY FLORIDA 2210 Executive Drive Salisbury NORTH CAROLINA 28147

Dear Reader,

If you enjoyed reading Czechmate, I would appreciate it if you would help others enjoy this book, too. Here are some of the ways you can help spread the word:

Lend it. This book is lending enabled so please share it with a friend.

Recommend it. Help other readers find this book by recommending it to friends, readers' groups, book clubs, and discussion forums.

Share it. Let other readers know you've read the book by positing a note to your social media account and/or your Goodreads account.

Review it. Please tell others why you liked this book by reviewing it on your favorite ebook site like Amazon or Barnes and Noble and/or Goodreads.

Everything you do to help others learn about my book is greatly appreciated!

Felicia Bridges

Plan Your Next Escape!
What's Your Reading Pleasure?

Whether it's captivating historical romance, intriguing mysteries, young adult romance, illustrated children's books, or uplifting love stories, Vinspire Publishing has the adventure for you!

For a complete listing of books available, visit our website at www.vinspirepublishing.com.

Like us on Facebook at www.facebook.com/Vinspire-Publishing

Follow us on Twitter at
www.twitter.com/vinspire2004

and join our newsletter for details of our upcoming releases, giveaways, and more! http://t.co/46UoTbVaWr

We are your travel guide to your next adventure!